OXFORD STUDENT TEXTS

Series Editor: Victor Lee

Chaucer: The Nun's Priest's Tale

Geoffrey Chaucer
The Nun's Priest's Tale

Edited by
Peter Mack and Andy Hawkins

Oxford University Press

OXFORD
UNIVERSITY PRESS

Great Clarendon Street, Oxford OX2 6DP

Oxford University Press is a department of the University of Oxford.
It furthers the University's objective of excellence in research, scholarship,
and education by publishing worldwide in

Oxford New York

Auckland Cape Town Dar es Salaam Hong Kong Karachi
Kuala Lumpur Madrid Melbourne Mexico City Nairobi
New Delhi Shanghai Taipei Toronto

With offices in

Argentina Austria Brazil Chile Czech Republic France Greece
Guatemala Hungary Italy Japan South Korea Poland Portugal
Singapore Switzerland Thailand Turkey Ukraine Vietnam

Oxford is a registered trade mark of Oxford University Press
in the UK and in certain other countries

British Library Cataloguing in Publication Data

Data available

ISBN: 978-0-19-832548-2

3 5 7 9 10 8 6 4 2

Typeset by Palimpsest Book Production Ltd, Grangemouth, Stirlingshire
Printed in Great Britain by Cox and Wyman Ltd, Reading

The Publishers would like to thank the following for permission to
reproduce photographs:

Px Mary Evans Picture Library; p3 Corpus Christie College Cambridge/Oxford University
Press; p6 Mary Evans Picture Library; p93 The British Library; Department of Western
Manuscripts, Bodleian Library, Oxford; p97 Ken Harvey; p128 Robbie Munn/Rochester
Cathedral. The illustration on p43 is by Jeff Edwards

Contents

Acknowledgements viii

Editors viii

Foreword ix

Chaucer's *Nun's Priest's Tale* in Context 1

The Nun's Priest's Tale 7
The Nun's Priest's Prologue 7
The Nun's Priest's Tale 9
Epilogue to The Nun's Priest's Tale 28

Notes 29
The Nun's Priest's Prologue 31
The Knight interrupts The Monk: lines 1–25 31
The Host speaks to The Monk and The Nun's Priest:
    lines 26–54 33

The Nun's Priest's Tale 37
A description of the poor widow: lines 55–80 39
A description of Chauntecleer: lines 81–98 41
Chauntecleer's hens: lines 99–115 44
Chauntecleer's dream: lines 116–41 46
Pertelote responds to Chauntecleer's dream:
    lines 142–203 47
Chauntecleer begins his reply: lines 204–17 52
Chauntecleer's first story: lines 218–96 53
Chauntecleer's second story: lines 297–343 56
Chauntecleer cites more examples and authorities:
    lines 344–90 58
Chauntecleer is overcome by Pertelote's beauty:
    lines 391–420 61
Chauntecleer's precarious happiness: lines 421–48 62
The fox lies in wait for Chauntecleer: lines 449–63 65

The Nun's Priest on dreams and predestination:
    lines 464–84   67
The Nun's Priest on women's advice: lines 485–500   70
Chauntecleer notices the fox: lines 501–15   71
The fox's flattering speech: lines 516–64   72
The fox seizes Chauntecleer: lines 565–608   74
Everyone chases the fox: lines 609–35   77
Chauntecleer's escape and the moral of the tale:
    lines 636–80   79

Epilogue to The Nun's Priest's Tale   84
The Host congratulates The Nun's Priest on his tale:
    lines 681–96   84

Interpretations   87
Setting and genre   87
Setting the tale in context   87
The link between *The Monk's Tale* and *The Nun's Priest's
Tale*   89
Genre   90
The beast-fable   91
The heroic and the mock-heroic   97
Realism   99
The 'mixed style'   100

Structure, language and style   102
Narrative and narrators   102
Rhetoric   106

Ideas and themes   110
Dreams   110
Attitudes to women   114
Relationships between men and women   117
Taketh the moralite...   120
The Epilogue   123

Critical views   124

Essay Questions 127

Chronology 131

Further Reading 135

A Note on Chaucer's English 139

A Note on Pronunciation 147

Glossary 149

Appendix 159
The description of The Prioress 159
Chauntecleer's first story 162
A beast-fable from Aesop 163
A summary of the story of Reynard and Chantecler 164

Acknowledgements

Peter Mack would like to acknowledge the help he received in compiling the Notes from the critical works and editions listed in Further Reading, and from his colleagues, Gloria Cigman and Bill Whitehead. He is grateful to Robert Burchfield for his comments on the Note on Chaucer's English. Thanks are also due to Marion Blandford for advice on the habits of chickens. Andy Hawkins would like to thank former A-level students from Ysgol Gyfun Llangefni for their insights into *The Nun's Priest's Tale* and colleagues in Powys for their comments on the Interpretations. Both editors would like to thank Victor Lee and Lucy Hooper for their constructive criticism and advice. The text is taken from L. D. Benson (ed.), *The Riverside Chaucer* (Cambridge, Mass., 1987), with permission.

Editors

Dr Victor Lee, the series editor, read English at University College, Cardiff. He was later awarded his doctorate at the University of Oxford. He has taught at secondary and tertiary level, working at the Open University for 27 years. Victor Lee's experience as an examiner is very wide. He has been, for example, a Chief Examiner in English A-level for three different boards, stretching over a period of more than 30 years.

Professor Peter Mack read English at St Peter's College, Oxford, and went on to gain an MPhil and PhD in Renaissance Studies from The Warburg Institute, University of London. He has examined English at GCSE and A level as well as for the International Baccalaureate. He has been Editor of the journal *Rhetorica* and Head of the English Department at the University of Warwick, where he has taught Medieval English Studies since 1979. His books include *Renaissance Argument* (1993), *Renaissance Rhetoric* (1994) and *Elizabethan Rhetoric* (2002).

Andy Hawkins read English at the University of Wales, Bangor, where she also gained her MA. She has extensive teaching and examining experience and has also worked as an English adviser in Powys. Her work includes the development of alternative approaches to texts and creative writing for A-level coursework. She is also an editor of poetry books for children, including *Thoughts Like an Ocean* (1997), *Look Out* (1999) and *Second Thoughts* (2003).

Foreword

Oxford Student Texts are specifically aimed at presenting poetry and drama to an audience studying English literature at an advanced level. Each text is designed as an integrated whole consisting of four main parts. The first part sets the scene by discussing the context in which the work was written. The most important part of the book is the poetry or play itself, and it is suggested that the student reads this first without consulting the Notes or other secondary sources. To encourage students to follow this advice, the Notes are placed together after the text, not alongside it. Where help is needed, the Notes and Interpretations sections provide it.

The Notes perform two functions. First, they provide information and explain allusions. Second (this is where they differ from most texts at this level), they often raise questions of central concern to the interpretation of the poems or play being dealt with, particularly in the general note placed at the beginning of each set of notes.

The fourth part, the Interpretations section, deals with major issues of response to the particular selection of poetry or drama. One of the major aims of this part of the text is to emphasize that there is no one right answer to interpretation, but a series of approaches. Readers are given guidance as to what counts as evidence, but in the end left to make up their own minds as to which are the most suitable interpretations, or to add their own.

In these revised editions, the Interpretations section now addresses a wider range of issues. There is a more detailed treatment of context and critical history, for example. The section contains a number of activity-discussion sequences, although it must be stressed that these are optional. Significant issues about the poetry or play are raised, and readers are invited to tackle activities before proceeding to the discussion section, where possible responses to the questions raised are considered. Their main function is to engage readers actively in the ideas of the text.

At the end of each text there is also a list of Essay Questions. Whereas the activity-discussion sequences are aimed at increasing understanding of the literary work itself, these tasks are intended to help explore ideas about the poetry or play after the student has completed the reading of the work and the studying of the Notes and Interpretations. These tasks are particularly helpful for coursework projects or in preparing for an examination.

Victor Lee *Series Editor*

CHAUCER.

A woodcut based on a portrait miniature of Chaucer from the Ellesmere manuscript of *The Canterbury Tales*. The manuscript was copied and illustrated a few years after Chaucer's death.

Chaucer's *Nun's Priest's Tale* in Context

Conditions of writing

During Chaucer's lifetime (*c.*1343–1400), and for two centuries afterwards, it was impossible to make a living by writing. In order to support themselves writers needed other jobs (Chaucer worked as a diplomat and a civil servant; some other writers worked as priests) and patronage, which usually took the form of money in return for the dedication of a poem or a book or the gift of a manuscript copy. The only people with the financial resources to provide writers with patronage were the King, the great barons of the realm and, increasingly in the fourteenth and fifteenth centuries, wealthy London merchants.

Chaucer was the son of a London wine merchant. As a child at home, he would have learned to read and write English and French. He may have also learned Italian from his father's business associates. At school he was taught Latin, which was the language of learning and of much international communication. The young Chaucer would also have learned rhetoric, which was the art of speaking and writing effectively. In 1357, at the age of about fourteen, Chaucer became a page in the household of Elizabeth, Countess of Ulster, and Prince Lionel, King Edward III's second son. Then in 1359 he was sent to France as a squire in the English army. So Chaucer combined a London mercantile origin and basic education with the training and early manhood experiences of a courtier.

In the fourteenth century, it was relatively expensive to own a manuscript (and of course manuscripts were the only kind of books before the invention of printing around 1465). Usually you had to borrow a copy of the work you wanted, buy parchment and ink and hire a scribe to copy it out for you. Some booksellers hired scribes to make ready-to-buy copies of books they thought would sell, but the cost of this service was higher.

Few people knew how to read and write, or had the leisure to do so. In great courts a poet might read from his book to the nobles, their feudal supporters and their servants. The feudal system of land tenure meant that great lords held their lands in return for military service to and attendance on the King. In the same way, lesser feudal lords would owe service to their superiors and expect service and attendance from the knights and squires dependent on them. Merchant families who were sufficiently wealthy to afford books for leisure may have imitated courtly practice with after-meal readings of poetry to the whole family, or family members may have read to themselves.

Because the main sources of patronage were aristocratic, non-religious literature tends to employ aristocratic forms, like the romance, and to uphold aristocratic values. Since the great merchants aspired to (and sometimes did) join the aristocracy they would have followed aristocratic tastes but they may have been more willing to entertain mockery or criticism of, for example, aristocratic complacency and idleness. Although merchants, like Chaucer's father, made much of their money from paid service to the King and nobles, their position was ultimately reliant on the financial profits they could make. They were both partly independent of the state and more reliant than aristocrats on their own ability to respond quickly to the challenges and opportunities of the international market.

There is some manuscript and historical evidence that whereas Chaucer's earlier poems, such as *The Book of the Duchess* and *Troilus and Criseyde*, were directed to royal or aristocratic patrons, *The Canterbury Tales*, which he wrote towards the end of his career and left incomplete at his death, was intended for a London business audience. This would have been a good reason for adding representatives of various trades to the pilgrims, as he does in the *General Prologue*. For a courtly audience it would have seemed strange to write about a large group of people which included only one knight and his squire.

This fifteenth-century manuscript of Chaucer's *Troilus and Criseyde* apparently shows Chaucer (in the centre) reading his poem to the court of Richard II. A colour version of the illustration can be seen on www.sas.upenn.edu/~jhsy/chaucer-troilus.html.

Genre and ideas

If Chaucer did indeed direct *The Canterbury Tales* to a new, less aristocratic, more urban audience, this might explain why he felt able to take an amused and critical approach to genre. *The Nun's Priest's Tale* is a beast-fable, a perfectly respectable medieval genre for moral teaching (see Interpretations, p. 91). However, Chaucer adds to this both mock-heroic (see Interpretations, p. 97), which makes fun of the conventions of aristocratic poetry by applying them inappropriately, and a series of jokes about the moral meaning of stories. So the form and tone of *The Nun's Priest's Tale* may reflect the greater freedom which Chaucer felt in writing primarily for a non-aristocratic audience.

Furthermore, *The Nun's Priest's Tale* provides a light-hearted view of some widely accepted medieval theories, such as the theory of the four humours and certain medical remedies based on it, and contemporary debates, for example about the significance of dreams and whether God's foreknowledge of events implies predestination. (See Interpretations, pp. 110.) Chaucer's poem implies an audience which is well-informed but which is also willing to laugh at theories and debates which some people took seriously. The way in which the poem jokes about the medieval practice of telling stories to exemplify an established moral truth may imply an audience willing to laugh at or question traditional moral attitudes.

The Peasants' Revolt

In June 1381, an army of peasants and craftsmen from Kent marched on London to protest against their poverty and the excessive taxes imposed on them. They sacked John of Gaunt's palace at the Savoy because they held him responsible for the new taxes and killed some prominent royal officials, including the Archbishop of Canterbury and the Lord Treasurer, and many foreigners. Chaucer, himself a royal official, was present in London, living in his apartment over Aldgate while these disturbing events were going on. The Flemish people murdered by the rebels came from the part of town and the community Chaucer grew up in. The only reference to the revolt in Chaucer's writing occurs in *The Nun's Priest's Tale*, when the villagers running after the fox are rather ludicrously said to be much louder than Jack Straw (one of the leaders of the revolt) and his crowd when they went about killing the Flemish (lines 628–31). It is extraordinary that Chaucer, writing only ten to fifteen years later, can show so much detachment from these terrible events which he clearly remembers so well.

The Nun's Priest

Chaucer deliberately makes the teller of his tale a person of some learning who can be expected to know the positions of contemporary thinkers on dreams and predestination and hold views of his own on these subjects. The Nun's Priest was one of three priests accompanying The Prioress, who is depicted as an aristocratic lady who has become a nun, possibly because her family did not wish to pay a large dowry to her husband if she were to get married. In terms of learning and church position, as a priest he is her superior but socially he is inferior to her and economically he is dependent on her good will for his continued employment. In a world in which men expected to dominate their wives and daughters and in which literature frequently emphasized male superiority and endorsed unfair criticism of women, his position is distinctly ambivalent. As a learned man and a priest he expects to be in control. His deviously critical comments on women (which he partly withdraws) suggest both that he resents his position of dependence and that he understands that he has insufficient power and security to express his resentment openly. *The Nun's Priest's Tale*'s ambiguous and mocking attitude to authority may reflect either Chaucer's understanding of The Nun's Priest's difficult social position or his own realization that the patronage power of the London merchants opened up possibilities of questioning the social and intellectual order of feudalism.

These woodcuts were based on miniature portraits in the Ellesmere manuscript. Notice the elaborate trappings of The Prioress's horse (left), and The Monk's bells and hunting dogs (below).

The Nun's Priest's Tale

The Nun's Priest's Prologue
The prologe of the Nonnes Preestes Tale.

> 'Hoo!' quod the Knyght, 'good sire, namoore of this!
> That ye han seyd is right ynough, ywis,
> And muchel moore; for litel hevynesse
> Is right ynough to muche folk, I gesse.
> 5 I seye for me, it is a greet disese,
> Whereas men han been in greet welthe and ese,
> To heeren of hire sodeyn fal, allas!
> And the contrarie is joye and greet solas,
> As whan a man hath been in povre estaat,
> 10 And clymbeth up and wexeth fortunat,
> And there abideth in prosperitee.
> Swich thyng is gladsom, as it thynketh me,
> And of swich thyng were goodly for to telle.'
>   'Ye,' quod oure Hooste, 'by Seint Poules belle!
> 15 Ye seye right sooth; this Monk he clappeth lowde.
> He spak how Fortune covered with a clowde
> I noot nevere what; and als of a tragedie
> Right now ye herde, and pardee, no remedie
> It is for to biwaille ne compleyne
> 20 That that is doon, and als it is a peyne,
> As ye han seyd, to heere of hevynesse.
>   'Sire Monk, namoore of this, so God yow blesse!
> Youre tale anoyeth al this compaignye.
> Swich talkyng is nat worth a boterflye,
> 25 For therinne is ther no desport ne game.
> Wherfore, sire Monk, daun Piers by youre name,
> I pray yow hertely telle us somwhat elles;

For sikerly, nere clynkyng of youre belles
That on youre bridel hange on every syde,
30 By hevene kyng that for us alle dyde,
I sholde er this han fallen doun for sleep,
Althogh the slough had never been so deep;
Thanne hadde your tale al be toold in veyn.
For certeinly, as that thise clerkes seyn,
35 Whereas a man may have noon audience,
Noght helpeth it to tellen his sentence.
   'And wel I woot the substance is in me,
If any thyng shal wel reported be.
Sir, sey somwhat of huntyng, I yow preye.'
40   'Nay,' quod this Monk, 'I have no lust to pleye.
Now lat another telle, as I have toold.'
Thanne spak oure Hoost with rude speche and boold,
And seyde unto the Nonnes Preest anon,
'Com neer, thou preest, com hyder, thou sir John!
45 Telle us swich thyng as may oure hertes glade.
Be blithe, though thou ryde upon a jade.
What thogh thyn hors be bothe foul and lene?
If he wol serve thee, rekke nat a bene.
Looke that thyn herte be murie everemo.'
50   'Yis, sir,' quod he, 'yis, Hoost, so moot I go,
But I be myrie, ywis I wol be blamed.'
And right anon his tale he hath attamed,
And thus he seyde unto us everichon,
This sweete preest, this goodly man sir John.

The Nun's Priest's Tale

Heere bigynneth the Nonnes Preestes Tale of the Cok and Hen, Chauntecleer and Pertelote.

55   A povre wydwe, somdeel stape in age,
    Was whilom dwellyng in a narwe cotage,
    Biside a grove, stondynge in a dale.
    This wydwe, of which I telle yow my tale,
    Syn thilke day that she was last a wyf
60   In pacience ladde a ful symple lyf,
    For litel was hir catel and hir rente.
    By housbondrie of swich as God hire sente
    She foond hirself and eek hir doghtren two.
    Thre large sowes hadde she, and namo,
65   Three keen, and eek a sheep that highte Malle.
    Ful sooty was hire bour and eek hir halle,
    In which she eet ful many a sklendre meel.
    Of poynaunt sauce hir neded never a deel.
    No deyntee morsel passed thurgh hir throte;
70   Hir diete was accordant to hir cote.
    Repleccioun ne made hire nevere sik;
    Attempree diete was al hir phisik,
    And exercise, and hertes suffisaunce.
    The goute lette hire nothyng for to daunce,
75   N'apoplexie shente nat hir heed.
    No wyn ne drank she, neither whit ne reed;
    Hir bord was served moost with whit and blak –
    Milk and broun breed, in which she foond no lak,
    Seynd bacoun, and somtyme an ey or tweye,
80   For she was, as it were, a maner deye.
    A yeerd she hadde, enclosed al aboute
    With stikkes, and a drye dych withoute,
    In which she hadde a cok, hight Chauntecleer.

In al the land, of crowyng nas his peer.
85 His voys was murier than the murie orgon
On messe-dayes that in the chirche gon.
Wel sikerer was his crowyng in his logge
Than is a clokke or an abbey orlogge.
By nature he knew ech ascencioun
90 Of the equynoxial in thilke toun;
For whan degrees fiftene weren ascended,
Thanne crew he that it myghte nat been amended.
His coomb was redder than the fyn coral,
And batailled as it were a castel wal;
95 His byle was blak, and as the jeet it shoon;
Lyk asure were his legges and his toon;
His nayles whitter than the lylye flour,
And lyk the burned gold was his colour.
This gentil cok hadde in his governaunce
100 Sevene hennes for to doon al his plesaunce,
Whiche were his sustres and his paramours,
And wonder lyk to hym, as of colours;
Of whiche the faireste hewed on hir throte
Was cleped faire damoysele Pertelote.
105 Curteys she was, discreet, and debonaire,
And compaignable, and bar hyrself so faire
Syn thilke day that she was seven nyght oold
That trewely she hath the herte in hoold
Of Chauntecleer, loken in every lith;
110 He loved hire so that wel was hym therwith.
But swich a joye was it to here hem synge,
Whan that the brighte sonne gan to sprynge,
In sweete accord, 'My lief is faren in londe!' –
For thilke tyme, as I have understonde,
115 Beestes and briddes koude speke and synge.
    And so bifel that in a dawenynge,
As Chauntecleer among his wyves alle
Sat on his perche, that was in the halle,

And next hym sat this faire Pertelote,
120 This Chauntecleer gan gronen in his throte,
As man that in his dreem is drecched soore.
And whan that Pertelote thus herde hym roore,
She was agast and seyde, 'Herte deere,
What eyleth yow, to grone in this manere?
125 Ye been a verray sleper; fy, for shame!'
    And he answerde, and seyde thus: 'Madame,
I pray yow that ye take it nat agrief.
By God, me mette I was in swich meschief
Right now that yet myn herte is soore afright.
130 Now God,' quod he, 'my swevene recche aright,
And kepe my body out of foul prisoun!
Me mette how that I romed up and doun
Withinne our yeerd, wheer as I saugh a beest
Was lyk an hound, and wolde han maad areest
135 Upon my body, and wolde han had me deed.
His colour was bitwixe yelow and reed,
And tipped was his tayl and bothe his eeris
With blak, unlyk the remenant of his heeris;
His snowte smal, with glowynge eyen tweye.
140 Yet of his look for feere almoost I deye;
This caused me my gronyng, doutelees.'
    'Avoy!' quod she, 'fy on yow, hertelees!
Allas,' quod she, 'for, by that God above,
Now han ye lost myn herte and al my love!
145 I kan nat love a coward, by my feith!
For certes, what so any womman seith,
We alle desiren, if it myghte bee,
To han housbondes hardy, wise, and free,
And secree – and no nygard, ne no fool,
150 Ne hym that is agast of every tool,
Ne noon avauntour, by that God above!
How dorste ye seyn, for shame, unto youre love
That any thyng myghte make yow aferd?

Have ye no mannes herte, and han a berd?
155   Allas! And konne ye been agast of swevenys?
Nothyng, God woot, but vanitee in sweven is.
Swevenes engendren of replecciouns,
And ofte of fume and of complecciouns,
Whan humours been to habundant in a wight.
160   Certes this dreem, which ye han met to-nyght,
Cometh of the greete superfluytee
Of youre rede colera, pardee,
Which causeth folk to dreden in hir dremes
Of arwes, and of fyr with rede lemes,
165   Of rede beestes, that they wol hem byte,
Of contek, and of whelpes, grete and lyte;
Right as the humour of malencolie
Causeth ful many a man in sleep to crie
For feere of blake beres, or boles blake,
170   Or elles blake develes wole hem take.
Of othere humours koude I telle also
That werken many a man sleep ful wo;
But I wol passe as lightly as I kan.
    'Lo Catoun, which that was so wys a man,
175   Seyde he nat thus, "Ne do no fors of dremes"?
    'Now sire,' quod she, 'whan we flee fro the bemes,
For Goddes love, as taak som laxatyf.
Up peril of my soule and of my lyf,
I conseille yow the beste – I wol nat lye –
180   That bothe of colere and of malencolye
Ye purge yow; and for ye shal nat tarie,
Though in this toun is noon apothecarie,
I shal myself to herbes techen yow
That shul been for youre hele and for youre prow;
185   And in oure yeerd tho herbes shal I fynde
The whiche han of hire propretee by kynde
To purge yow bynethe and eek above.
Foryet nat this, for Goddes owene love!

Ye been ful coleryk of compleccioun;
190 Ware the sonne in his ascencioun
Ne fynde yow nat repleet of humours hoote.
And if it do, I dar wel leye a grote,
That ye shul have a fevere terciane,
Or an agu that may be youre bane.
195 A day or two ye shul have digestyves
Of wormes, er ye take youre laxatyves
Of lawriol, centaure, and fumetere,
Or elles of ellebor, that groweth there,
Of katapuce, or of gaitrys beryis,
200 Of herbe yve, growyng in oure yeerd, ther mery is;
Pekke hem up right as they growe and ete hem yn.
Be myrie, housbonde, for youre fader kyn!
Dredeth no dreem; I kan sey yow namoore.'
    'Madame,' quod he, 'graunt mercy of youre loore.
205 But nathelees, as touchyng daun Catoun,
That hath of wysdom swich a greet renoun,
Though that he bad no dremes for to drede,
By God, men may in olde bookes rede
Of many a man moore of auctorite
210 Than evere Caton was, so moot I thee,
That al the revers seyn of this sentence,
And han wel founden by experience
That dremes been significaciouns
As wel of joye as of tribulaciouns
215 That folk enduren in this lif present.
Ther nedeth make of this noon argument;
The verray preeve sheweth it in dede.
    'Oon of the gretteste auctour that men rede
Seith thus: that whilom two felawes wente
220 On pilgrimage, in a ful good entente,
And happed so, they coomen in a toun
Wher as ther was swich congregacioun
Of peple, and eek so streit of herbergage,

That they ne founde as muche as o cotage
225 In which they bothe myghte ylogged bee.
Wherfore they mosten of necessitee,
As for that nyght, departen compaignye;
And ech of hem gooth to his hostelrye,
And took his loggyng as it wolde falle.
230 That oon of hem was logged in a stalle,
Fer in a yeerd, with oxen of the plough;
That oother man was logged wel ynough,
As was his aventure or his fortune,
That us governeth alle as in commune.
235   'And so bifel that, longe er it were day,
This man mette in his bed, ther as he lay,
How that his felawe gan upon hym calle,
And seyde, "Allas, for in an oxes stalle
This nyght I shal be mordred ther I lye!
240 Now help me, deere brother, or I dye.
In alle haste com to me!" he sayde.
This man out of his sleep for feere abrayde;
But whan that he was wakened of his sleep,
He turned hym and took of this no keep.
245 Hym thoughte his dreem nas but a vanitee.
Thus twies in his slepyng dremed hee;
And atte thridde tyme yet his felawe
Cam, as hym thoughte, and seide, "I am now slawe.
Bihoold my bloody woundes depe and wyde!
250 Arys up erly in the morwe tyde,
And at the west gate of the toun," quod he,
"A carte ful of dong ther shaltow se,
In which my body is hid ful prively;
Do thilke carte arresten boldely.
255 My gold caused my mordre, sooth to sayn,"
And tolde hym every point how he was slayn,
With a ful pitous face, pale of hewe.
And truste wel, his dreem he foond ful trewe,

For on the morwe, as soone as it was day,
260 To his felawes in he took the way;
And whan that he cam to this oxes stalle,
After his felawe he bigan to calle.
   'The hostiler answerede hym anon,
And seyde, "Sire, your felawe is agon.
265 As soone as day he wente out of the toun."
   'This man gan fallen in suspecioun,
Remembrynge on his dremes that he mette,
And forth he gooth – no lenger wolde he lette –
Unto the west gate of the toun, and fond
270 A dong-carte, wente as it were to donge lond,
That was arrayed in that same wise
As ye han herd the dede man devyse.
And with an hardy herte he gan to crye
Vengeance and justice of this felonye:
275 "My felawe mordred is this same nyght,
And in this carte he lith gapyng upright.
I crye out on the ministres," quod he,
"That sholden kepe and reulen this citee.
Harrow! Allas! Heere lith my felawe slayn!"
280 What sholde I moore unto this tale sayn?
The peple out sterte and caste the cart to grounde,
And in the myddel of the dong they founde
The dede man, that mordred was al newe.
   'O blisful God, that art so just and trewe,
285 Lo, how that thou biwreyest mordre alway!
Mordre wol out; that se we day by day.
Mordre is so wlatsom and abhomynable
To God, that is so just and resonable,
That he ne wol nat suffre it heled be,
290 Though it abyde a yeer, or two, or thre.
Mordre wol out, this my conclusioun.
And right anon, ministres of that toun
Han hent the carter and so soore hym pyned,

15

And eek the hostiler so soore engyned,
295 That they biknewe hire wikkednesse anon,
And were anhanged by the nekke-bon.
    'Heere may men seen that dremes been to drede.
And certes in the same book I rede,
Right in the nexte chapitre after this –
300 I gabbe nat, so have I joye or blis –
Two men that wolde han passed over see,
For certeyn cause, into a fer contree,
If that the wynd ne hadde been contrarie,
That made hem in a citee for to tarie
305 That stood ful myrie upon an haven-syde;
But on a day, agayn the even-tyde,
The wynd gan chaunge, and blew right as hem leste.
Jolif and glad they wente unto hir reste,
And casten hem ful erly for to saille.
310 But herkneth! To that o man fil a greet mervaille:
That oon of hem, in slepyng as he lay,
Hym mette a wonder dreem agayn the day.
Hym thoughte a man stood by his beddes syde,
And hym comanded that he sholde abyde,
315 And seyde hym thus: "If thou tomorwe wende,
Thow shalt be dreynt; my tale is at an ende."
He wook, and tolde his felawe what he mette,
And preyde hym his viage for to lette;
As for that day, he preyde hym to byde.
320 His felawe, that lay by his beddes syde,
Gan for to laughe, and scorned him ful faste.
"No dreem," quod he, "may so myn herte agaste
That I wol lette for to do my thynges.
I sette nat a straw by thy dremynges,
325 For swevenes been but vanytees and japes.
Men dreme alday of owles and of apes,
And of many a maze therwithal;
Men dreme of thyng that nevere was ne shal.

But sith I see that thou wolt heere abyde,
330 And thus forslewthen wilfully thy tyde,
God woot, it reweth me; and have good day!"
And thus he took his leve, and wente his way.
But er that he hadde half his cours yseyled,
Noot I nat why, ne what myschaunce it eyled,
335 But casuelly the shippes botme rente,
And ship and man under the water wente
In sighte of othere shippes it bisyde,
That with hem seyled at the same tyde.
And therfore, faire Pertelote so deere,
340 By swiche ensamples olde maistow leere
That no man sholde been to recchelees
Of dremes; for I seye thee, doutelees,
That many a dreem ful soore is for to drede.
    'Lo, in the lyf of Seint Kenelm I rede,
345 That was Kenulphus sone, the noble kyng
Of Mercenrike, how Kenelm mette a thyng.
A lite er he was mordred, on a day,
His mordre in his avysioun he say.
His norice hym expowned every deel
350 His sweven, and bad hym for to kepe hym weel
For traisoun; but he nas but seven yeer oold,
And therfore litel tale hath he toold
Of any dreem, so hooly was his herte.
By God! I hadde levere than my sherte
355 That ye hadde rad his legende, as have I.
    'Dame Pertelote, I sey yow trewely,
Macrobeus, that writ the avisioun
In Affrike of the worthy Cipioun,
Affermeth dremes, and seith that they been
360 Warnynge of thynges that men after seen.
And forthermoore, I pray yow, looketh wel
In the olde testament, of Daniel,
If he heeld dremes any vanitee.

Reed eek of Joseph, and ther shul ye see
365 Wher dremes be somtyme – I sey nat alle –
Warnynge of thynges that shul after falle.
Looke of Egipte the kyng, daun Pharao,
His bakere and his butiller also,
Wher they ne felte noon effect in dremes.
370 Whoso wol seken actes of sondry remes
May rede of dremes many a wonder thyng.
Lo Cresus, which that was of Lyde kyng,
Mette he nat that he sat upon a tree,
Which signified he sholde anhanged bee?
375 Lo heere Andromacha, Ectores wyf,
That day that Ector sholde lese his lyf,
She dremed on the same nyght biforn
How that the lyf of Ector sholde be lorn,
If thilke day he wente into bataille.
380 She warned hym, but it myghte nat availle;
He wente for to fighte natheles,
But he was slayn anon of Achilles.
But thilke tale is al to longe to telle,
And eek it is ny day; I may nat dwelle.
385 Shortly I seye, as for conclusioun,
That I shal han of this avisioun
Adversitee; and I seye forthermoor
That I ne telle of laxatyves no stoor,
For they been venymes, I woot it weel;
390 I hem diffye, I love hem never a deel!
    'Now let us speke of myrthe, and stynte al this.
Madame Pertelote, so have I blis,
Of o thyng God hath sent me large grace;
For whan I se the beautee of youre face,
395 Ye been so scarlet reed aboute youre yen,
It maketh al my drede for to dyen;
For al so siker as In *principio*,
Mulier est hominis confusio –

Madame, the sentence of this Latyn is,
400 "Womman is mannes joye and al his blis."
For whan I feele a-nyght your softe syde –
Al be it that I may nat on yow ryde,
For that oure perche is maad so narwe, allas –
I am so ful of joye and of solas,
405 That I diffye bothe sweven and dreem.'
      And with that word he fley doun fro the beem,
For it was day, and eke his hennes alle,
And with a chuk he gan hem for to calle,
For he hadde founde a corn, lay in the yerd.
410 Real he was, he was namoore aferd.
He fethered Pertelote twenty tyme,
And trad hire eke as ofte, er it was pryme.
He looketh as it were a grym leoun,
And on his toos he rometh up and doun;
415 Hym deigned nat to sette his foot to grounde.
He chukketh whan he hath a corn yfounde,
And to hym rennen thanne his wyves alle.
Thus roial, as a prince is in his halle,
Leve I this Chauntecleer in his pasture,
420 And after wol I telle his aventure.
      Whan that the month in which the world bigan,
That highte March, whan God first maked man,
Was compleet, and passed were also,
Syn March [was gon], thritty dayes and two,
425 Bifel that Chauntecleer in al his pryde,
His sevene wyves walkynge by his syde,
Caste up his eyen to the brighte sonne,
That in the signe of Taurus hadde yronne
Twenty degrees and oon, and somwhat moore,
430 And knew by kynde, and by noon oother loore,
That it was pryme, and crew with blisful stevene.
'The sonne,' he seyde, 'is clomben up on hevene
Fourty degrees and oon, and moore ywis.

Madame Pertelote, my worldes blis,
435 Herkneth thise blisful briddes how they synge,
And se the fresshe floures how they sprynge;
Ful is myn herte of revel and solas!'
But sodeynly hym fil a sorweful cas,
For evere the latter ende of joye is wo.
440 God woot that worldly joye is soone ago;
And if a rethor koude faire endite,
He in a cronycle saufly myghte it write
As for a sovereyn notabilitee.
Now every wys man, lat him herkne me;
445 This storie is also trewe, I undertake,
As is the book of Launcelot de Lake,
That wommen holde in ful greet reverence.
Now wol I torne agayn to my sentence.
    A col-fox, ful of sly iniquitee,
450 That in the grove hadde woned yeres three,
By heigh ymaginacioun forncast,
The same nyght thurghout the hegges brast
Into the yerd ther Chauntecleer the faire
Was wont, and eek his wyves, to repaire;
455 And in a bed of wortes stille he lay
Til it was passed undren of the day,
Waitynge his tyme on Chauntecleer to falle,
As gladly doon thise homycides alle
That in await liggen to mordre men.
460 O false mordrour, lurkynge in thy den!
O newe Scariot, newe Genylon,
False dissymulour, o Greek Synon,
That broghtest Troye al outrely to sorwe!
O Chauntecleer, acursed be that morwe
465 That thou into that yerd flaugh fro the bemes!
Thou were ful wel ywarned by thy dremes
That thilke day was perilous to thee;
But what that God forwoot moot nedes bee,

After the opinioun of certein clerkis.
470 Witnesse on hym that any parfit clerk is,
That in scole is greet altercacioun
In this mateere, and greet disputisoun,
And hath been of an hundred thousand men.
But I ne kan nat bulte it to the bren
475 As kan the hooly doctour Augustyn,
Or Boece, or the Bisshop Bradwardyn,
Wheither that Goddes worthy forwityng
Streyneth me nedely for to doon a thyng –
'Nedely' clepe I symple necessitee –
480 Or elles, if free choys be graunted me
To do that same thyng, or do it noght,
Though God forwoot it er that I was wroght;
Or if his wityng streyneth never a deel
But by necessitee condicioneel.
485 I wol nat han to do of swich mateere;
My tale is of a cok, as ye may heere,
That tok his conseil of his wyf, with sorwe,
To walken in the yerd upon that morwe
That he hadde met that dreem that I yow tolde.
490 Wommennes conseils been ful ofte colde;
Wommannes conseil broghte us first to wo
And made Adam fro Paradys to go,
Ther as he was ful myrie and wel at ese.
But for I noot to whom it myght displese,
495 If I conseil of wommen wolde blame,
Passe over, for I seyde it in my game.
Rede auctours, where they trete of swich mateere,
And what they seyn of wommen ye may heere.
Thise been the cokkes wordes, and nat myne;
500 I kan noon harm of no womman divyne.
    Faire in the soond, to bathe hire myrily,
Lith Pertelote, and alle hire sustres by,
Agayn the sonne, and Chauntecleer so free

Soong murier than the mermayde in the see
505 (For Phisiologus seith sikerly
How that they syngen wel and myrily).
And so bifel that, as he caste his ye
Among the wortes on a boterflye,
He was war of this fox, that lay ful lowe.
510 Nothyng ne liste hym thanne for to crowe,
But cride anon, 'Cok! cok!' and up he sterte
As man that was affrayed in his herte.
For natureelly a beest desireth flee
Fro his contrarie, if he may it see,
515 Though he never erst hadde seyn it with his ye.
This Chauntecleer, whan he gan hym espye,
He wolde han fled, but that the fox anon
Seyde, 'Gentil sire, allas, wher wol ye gon?
Be ye affrayed of me that am youre freend?
520 Now, certes, I were worse than a feend,
If I to yow wolde harm or vileynye!
I am nat come youre conseil for t'espye,
But trewely, the cause of my comynge
Was oonly for to herkne how that ye synge.
525 For trewely, ye have as myrie a stevene
As any aungel hath that is in hevene.
Therwith ye han in musyk moore feelynge
Than hadde Boece, or any that kan synge.
My lord youre fader – God his soule blesse! –
530 And eek youre mooder, of hire gentillesse,
Han in myn hous ybeen to my greet ese;
And certes, sire, ful fayn wolde I yow plese.
But, for men speke of syngyng, I wol seye –
So moote I brouke wel myne eyen tweye –
535 Save yow, I herde nevere man so synge
As dide youre fader in the morwenynge.
Certes, it was of herte, al that he song.
And for to make his voys the moore strong,

He wolde so peyne hym that with bothe his yen
540 He moste wynke, so loude he wolde cryen,
And stonden on his tiptoon therwithal,
And strecche forth his nekke long and smal.
And eek he was of swich discrecioun
That ther nas no man in no regioun
545 That hym in song or wisedom myghte passe.
I have wel rad in "Daun Burnel the Asse,"
Among his vers, how that ther was a cok,
For that a preestes sone yaf hym a knok
Upon his leg whil he was yong and nyce,
550 He made hym for to lese his benefice.
But certeyn, ther nys no comparisoun
Bitwixe the wisedom and discrecioun
Of youre fader and of his subtiltee.
Now syngeth, sire, for seinte charitee;
555 Lat se; konne ye youre fader countrefete?'
    This Chauntecleer his wynges gan to bete,
As man that koude his traysoun nat espie,
So was he ravysshed with his flaterie.
    Allas, ye lordes, many a fals flatour
560 Is in youre courtes, and many a losengeour,
That plesen yow wel moore, by my feith,
Than he that soothfastnesse unto yow seith.
Redeth Ecclesiaste of flaterye;
Beth war, ye lordes, of hir trecherye.
565   This Chauntecleer stood hye upon his toos,
Strecchynge his nekke, and heeld his eyen cloos,
And gan to crowe loude for the nones.
And daun Russell the fox stirte up atones,
And by the gargat hente Chauntecleer,
570 And on his bak toward the wode hym beer,
For yet ne was ther no man that hym sewed.
    O destinee, that mayst nat been eschewed!
Allas, that Chauntecleer fleigh fro the bemes!

Allas, his wyf ne roghte nat of dremes!
575 And on a Friday fil al this meschaunce.
     O Venus, that art goddesse of plesaunce,
Syn that thy servant was this Chauntecleer,
And in thy servyce dide al his poweer,
Moore for delit than world to multiplye,
580 Why woldestow suffre hym on thy day to dye?
     O Gaufred, deere maister soverayn,
That whan thy worthy kyng Richard was slayn
With shot, compleynedest his deeth so soore,
Why ne hadde I now thy sentence and thy loore,
585 The Friday for to chide, as diden ye?
For on a Friday, soothly, slayn was he.
Thanne wolde I shewe yow how that I koude pleyne
For Chauntecleres drede and for his peyne.
     Certes, swich cry ne lamentacion
590 Was nevere of ladyes maad whan Ylion
Was wonne, and Pirrus with his streite swerd,
Whan he hadde hent kyng Priam by the berd,
And slayn hym, as seith us *Eneydos*,
As maden alle the hennes in the clos,
595 Whan they had seyn of Chauntecleer the sighte.
But sovereynly dame Pertelote shrighte
Ful louder than dide Hasdrubales wyf,
Whan that hir housbonde hadde lost his lyf
And that the Romayns hadde brend Cartage.
600 She was so ful of torment and of rage
That wilfully into the fyr she sterte
And brende hirselven with a stedefast herte.
     O woful hennes, right so criden ye
As whan that Nero brende the citee
605 Of Rome cryden senatoures wyves
For that hir husbondes losten alle hir lyves –
Withouten gilt this Nero hath hem slayn.
Now wole I turne to my tale agayn.

This sely wydwe and eek hir doghtres two
610   Herden thise hennes crie and maken wo,
And out at dores stirten they anon,
And syen the fox toward the grove gon,
And bar upon his bak the cok away,
And cryden, 'Out! Harrow and weylaway!
615   Ha, ha! The fox!' and after hym they ran,
And eek with staves many another man.
Ran Colle oure dogge, and Talbot and Gerland,
And Malkyn, with a dystaf in hir hand;
Ran cow and calf, and eek the verray hogges,
620   So fered for the berkyng of the dogges
And shoutyng of the men and wommen eeke
They ronne so hem thoughte hir herte breeke.
They yolleden as feendes doon in helle;
The dokes cryden as men wolde hem quelle;
625   The gees for feere flowen over the trees;
Out of the hyve cam the swarm of bees.
So hydous was the noyse – a, benedicitee! –
Certes, he Jakke Straw and his meynee
Ne made nevere shoutes half so shrille
630   Whan that they wolden any Flemyng kille,
As thilke day was maad upon the fox.
Of bras they broghten bemes, and of box,
Of horn, of boon, in whiche they blewe and powped,
And therwithal they skriked and they howped.
635   It semed as that hevene sholde falle.
      Now, goode men, I prey yow herkneth alle:
Lo, how Fortune turneth sodeynly
The hope and pryde eek of hir enemy!
This cok, that lay upon the foxes bak,
640   In al his drede unto the fox he spak,
And seyde, 'Sire, if that I were as ye,
Yet sholde I seyn, as wys God helpe me,
"Turneth agayn, ye proude cherles alle!

A verray pestilence upon yow falle!
645 Now I am come unto the wodes syde;
Maugree youre heed, the cok shal heere abyde.
I wol hym ete, in feith, and that anon!" '
      The fox answerde, 'In feith, it shal be don.'
And as he spak that word, al sodeynly
650 This cok brak from his mouth delyverly,
And heighe upon a tree he fleigh anon.
And whan the fox saugh that the cok was gon,
'Allas!' quod he, 'O Chauntecleer, allas!
I have to yow,' quod he, 'ydoon trespas,
655 In as muche as I maked yow aferd
Whan I yow hente and broghte out of the yerd.
But, sire, I dide it in no wikke entente.
Com doun, and I shal telle yow what I mente;
I shal seye sooth to yow, God help me so!'
660   'Nay thanne,' quod he, 'I shrewe us bothe two.
And first I shrewe myself, bothe blood and bones,
If thou bigyle me ofter than ones.
Thou shalt namoore thurgh thy flaterye
Do me to synge and wynke with myn ye;
665 For he that wynketh, whan he sholde see,
Al wilfully, God lat him nevere thee!'
      'Nay,' quod the fox, 'but God yeve hym
meschaunce,
That is so undiscreet of governaunce
That jangleth whan he sholde holde his pees.'
670   Lo, swich it is for to be recchelees
And necligent, and truste on flaterye.
      But ye that holden this tale a folye,
As of a fox, or of a cok and hen,
Taketh the moralite, goode men.
675 For Seint Paul seith that al that writen is,
To oure doctrine it is ywrite, ywis;
Taketh the fruyt, and lat the chaf be stille.

Now, goode God, if that it be thy wille,
As seith my lord, so make us alle goode men,
680 And brynge us to his heighe blisse! Amen.

Heere is ended the Nonnes Preestes Tale.

Epilogue to The Nun's Priest's Tale

'Sire Nonnes Preest,' oure Hooste seide anoon,
'I-blessed be thy breche, and every stoon!
This was a murie tale of Chauntecleer.
But by my trouthe, if thou were seculer,
685 Thou woldest ben a trede-foul aright.
For if thou have corage as thou hast myght,
Thee were nede of hennes, as I wene,
Ya, moo than seven tymes seventene.
See, whiche braunes hath this gentil preest,
690 So gret a nekke, and swich a large breest!
He loketh as a sperhauk with his yen;
Him nedeth nat his colour for to dyen
With brasile ne with greyn of Portyngale.
Now, sire, faire falle yow for youre tale!'
695   And after that he, with ful merie chere,
Seide unto another, as ye shuln heere.

Notes

The Canterbury Tales is a collection of stories told by a group of people of different occupations who had met at the Tabard inn in Southwark before setting out on the pilgrimage to Canterbury. A pilgrimage was a journey to a saint's shrine, usually undertaken to benefit the pilgrim's soul, but some people went on pilgrimages for social reasons, or for the pleasure of travel. Chaucer's pilgrims decide to increase the pleasure of their journey by holding a storytelling competition, under the control of The Host, the landlord of the Tabard inn. Whoever tells the tales which give best instruction (*sentence*) and most enjoyment (*solas*) will win a free meal at a grand supper to be paid for by the other pilgrims. This scheme has wonderful psychological plausibility but it also results in an interesting set of contrasts. The pilgrims are competing with each other in telling stories, but they are collaborating in making the journey more enjoyable. Some are driven primarily by religious purposes, while others have secular pleasures in view. Some try to win the competition with the morality of their teaching, while others aim to amuse the company. *The Nun's Priest's Tale* highlights this contrast because it is a funny tale which invites us to question how seriously to take the moral teaching it offers.

The Canterbury Tales comprises three types of material: the tales, representing the different types of medieval story (such as romances, animal fables, moral stories and *fabliaux*); the *General Prologue*, which describes the pilgrims and outlines Chaucer's plan; and the link passages (such as *The Nun's Priest's Prologue*), in which the pilgrims react to the tale they have just heard and prepare for the next. In many of the tales one of our primary tasks is to compare the tale with the descriptions of the teller given in the *General Prologue* and the link passages. This is less of an issue in *The Nun's Priest's Tale* because we know nothing about the teller (apart from his employment) before he begins to tell his tale. But we must be concerned with the relationship between *The Nun's Priest's Tale* and other tales, especially its immediate predecessor, *The Monk's Tale*, because the link emphasizes the contrast between The Monk's gloomy stories and the tale the pilgrims now wish to hear. (See Interpretations, p. 89.)

The Nun's Priest's Prologue

The Knight interrupts The Monk: lines 1–25

The Monk's Tale had consisted of seventeen tragedies, the last of them that of Croesus, which ends with a description of tragedy:

> Tragediës noon oother maner thyng
> Ne kan in syngyng crie ne biwaille
> But that Fortune alwey wole assaille
> With unwar strook the regnes that been proude;
> For whan men trusteth hire, thanne wol she faille,
> And covere hire brighte face with a clowde.
>
> *(The Monk's Tale, 2761–6)*

At this The Knight interrupts The Monk, explaining that he has heard enough painful stories and would now prefer something more encouraging. The Host seconds his objection, picking up The Monk's words about Fortune and sorrow (16–20). Since these stories contain no pleasure or amusement (25), and in fact offend the company (23), they are worthless (24). What do these words tell us about The Host's response to tragedy? What qualities are The Knight and The Host looking for in stories? (See Interpretations, pp. 89–90).

There is good evidence that Chaucer rewrote this passage. The earlier version (preserved in the Hengwrt manuscript, the best of the early manuscripts) omitted lines 5–24 and gave a different version of line 25 (*Youre tales doon us no desport ne game*). In some manuscripts (though not in Hengwrt) the whole interruption is spoken by The Host. You might like to consider what Chaucer's later version (printed in our text from the Ellesmere manuscript, a very good manuscript slightly later than Hengwrt) adds to the depiction of his characters and his preparation for *The Nun's Priest's Tale*.

1 **Hoo** Stop.

   namoore no more. Since The Knight ranks highest among the
   pilgrims, it is appropriate that he should interrupt The Monk,
   who is also of high status (the *General Prologue* describes The
   Monk's fine clothes and horses, and calls him a *lord ful fat*
   [200]), on behalf of the other pilgrims. Notice that both The
   Knight and The Host show their respect by addressing The
   Monk as *sire* and using the polite form *ye* (see A Note on
   Chaucer's English, p. 139). The interruption may also reflect a
   difference of outlook. The Knight had told a tragic story of the
   love of two knights for a noble lady, but had brought about a
   happy ending in which the ravages of Fortune were overcome
   by the constancy of love and the wisdom of Theseus, the ruler
   of Athens.

2 What you have said is quite enough (*ynough*), indeed (*ywis*).

3 **muchel** much.

   hevynesse sadness, sorrow.

4 **muche** many.

   gesse guess, suppose.

5 **disese** sorrow, pain.

6–7 The Knight recalls the definition of tragedy from *The Monk's
   Prologue* (1973–77): a fall from great prosperity (*ese*) into misery.

8 **solas** comfort, pleasure.

9 **estaat** state, social position.

10 **wexeth** becomes.

   fortunat prosperous, favoured by Fortune. Fortune was
   worshipped as a goddess by the Romans. The late Roman
   author Boethius (about 480–524 AD) depicted Fortune as
   changeable, giving people wealth, power and prosperity, but
   also taking her gifts back again. He described this as climbing
   up one side of Fortune's wheel, only to be dashed down the
   other side. (See p. 128 for an illustration of 'The Wheel of
   Fortune'.) In *The Consolation of Philosophy*, a work which
   Chaucer translated and often used in his own writing, Boethius
   argued that people were better off when Fortune turned against
   them, because it was then that they discovered their true state
   and their real friends. The Knight finds it more comforting to
   hear of people blessed by Fortune.

12 **gladsom** pleasing.

it thynketh me it seems to me (the impersonal verb. See A Note on Chaucer's English, p. 139).

14 **Seint Poules belle** the bell of St Paul's Cathedral, the centre of civic life in the fourteenth century, when London was still a small, compact city.

15 **sooth** truth, truly.

clappeth chatters, babbles. The Host means to disparage the worth of what The Monk says. The word *clappeth* also picks up from the bell in the previous line.

16–17 The Host takes up the last words of *The Monk's Tale*. (See Notes, p. 31 and Note to line 10, p. 32.)

17 **I noot nevere what** I have no idea what. (For double negatives in Middle English, see A Note on Chaucer's English, p. 139.) Is The Host being truthful or dismissive here? What is the effect of his repeating The Monk's words?

18–20 **pardee… doon** by God, it is no help (*remedie*) to bewail and lament (*compleyne*) the thing that has happened. How does The Host's attitude to tragedy differ from The Knight's?

20 **als** also.

22 **so… blesse** as God may bless you.

23 **anoyeth** wearies, displeases.

24 **boterflye** butterfly (that is, 'is worth nothing at all'). Perhaps it is funny to compare something so ponderous as *The Monk's Tale* to a butterfly.

25 **desport** entertainment, pleasure.

game sport, enjoyment.

The Host speaks to The Monk and The Nun's Priest: lines 26–54

The Host says that he was so bored by *The Monk's Tale* that he almost fell asleep. If a storyteller cannot keep an audience interested he has no chance of putting across his teaching (35–6). The Host asks The Monk to tell another tale, preferably about hunting, but he refuses. So The Host asks The Nun's Priest to tell a merry tale, which he meekly agrees to do. Do you think it is rude, as Chaucer suggests (42), for The Host to call The Nun's Priest to him (44), tell him what kind of story to tell (45), and comment on the poor quality of his horse (46–7)? Why might The Host act rudely? (Notice Chaucer's expression of approval for The Nun's Priest [54].)

Some of The Host's remarks (28, 39) recall the description of The Monk in the *General Prologue* (165–207, specifically 169–71, 189), in which we learned that The Monk was a happy man who loved hunting and paid little attention to his monastic vows. The pilgrims may have been surprised that such a jolly, self-indulgent man should tell such sombre moral tales. Perhaps The Host remembers that he originally asked The Monk to tell the second tale (after *The Knight's Tale*, though the drunken Miller interrupted to prevent this) and therefore feels personally embarrassed by his disappointing performance. At all events his criticism of The Monk's storytelling is strong and personal.

26 **daun** master, sir (from Latin *dominus*). In *The Monk's Prologue* (3119–20), The Host made a point of not knowing The Monk's name, so it is possible that Piers is not his real name.

27 **elles** else.

28 **sikerly** certainly.
   nere (= *ne were*) were it not for.

30 By the King of heaven, who died for us all (i.e. by Jesus Christ).

31–2 Either: However deep the muddy holes (*slough*) (in the road) were, I should before now have fallen asleep, or: I should before now have fallen down (from the horse) because of sleep even though the mud (in the road) was deeper than ever. The first does not do much justice to *doun*, and involves the implication that the bumpy road would normally keep him awake (if the story were not so overpoweringly boring that only the bells did so). The second does not allow much role for *althogh*. Both insult The Monk's storytelling.

34 **clerkes** educated men, scholars.

35–36 This paraphrases Ecclesiasticus 32:6: *Do not waste your words where there is no one listening.* (Ecclesiasticus is a book of the Latin Bible, which Chaucer would have thought of as authoritative, but which Protestant scholars have relegated to the Apocrypha, a sort of appendix for books not accepted as fully belonging to the Bible.)

36 **sentence**   meaning.

37 **woot**   know.

substance   essence, heart of the matter. In his edition Sisam glossed this as 'stuff of a good listener', whereas Pollard takes it to refer to The Host's power of judging among the tales (*General Prologue*, 814). It might more easily mean 'the essence or teaching of a story'. The Host would be saying that if a story is well told he remembers its teaching.

38 **reported**   told.

39 Is The Host genuinely asking for another story or insulting The Monk by recalling the passion for hunting (which is against his monastic vows)?

40 **lust to pleye**   wish to indulge in games. Sexual meanings of *lust* (desire) and *pleye* (sexual activity) are also possible. The Host may have asked The Monk to describe his conquests (hunting) with The Monk replying in equally bawdy vein, though it hardly seems appropriate. This recalls The Host's banter in *The Monk's Prologue* (lines 1924–64) and the *Epilogue to The Nun's Priest's Tale* (see Notes to lines 681–96, pp. 84–5) where it seems better motivated. But neither The Monk nor The Nun's Priest replies in the same vein. It is possible that The Monk does not intend the puns here.

41 Now, since I have told mine, let someone else tell their tale.

43 *Nonnes Preest* implies that The Prioress only brought one priest with her. This contradicts the *preestes thre* mentioned in the *General Prologue* (164). This may represent a change of mind or the earlier passage may have been a mistake. One priest is more likely than three, but three is more ostentatious. It is also surely significant that Chaucer gives this important tale, with its discussion of the art of storytelling, to a pilgrim whom he has not described in the *General Prologue*. (See Interpretations, pp. 87–8.)

anon   at once.

44 **neer**   nearer. Notice that The Host uses the familiar *thou* to The Nun's Priest, whereas he used the more respectful *yow* (15, 22) to The Knight and The Monk. (See A Note on Chaucer's English, p. 139.)

45 **swich**   such.
   glade   gladden.
46 **blithe**   happy. Perhaps The Host comments on The Nun's
   Priest's nag (*jade*) as a critical comparison with The Monk's fine
   horse. Or perhaps he attacks the lower-ranking priest because
   he is fed up with deferring to the lordly Monk.
48 **rekke**   care.
49 **everemo**   always.
50 **so... go**   as I may thrive (an oath). *Yis* is the emphatic form of
   assent.
51 **But**   unless.
52 **attamed**   begun.
53 **everichon**   every one.

The Nun's Priest's Tale

Medieval stories were usually written to conform to certain types, or genres. An appreciation of the expectations aroused by the different genres (such as romance, *fabliau*, saint's life) is very important in understanding medieval storytelling. The predominant genre of *The Nun's Priest's Tale* is mock-heroic. (See Interpretations, pp. 97–9, which makes a comparison with Alexander Pope's poem, *The Rape of the Lock*.) Events and emotions are described in an inflated heroic style which is then deflated with the reminder that the story concerns a cock and his hens. This presents Chaucer with plenty of opportunities for exploiting his favourite literary device, the ironic gap between the language employed and the thing described. Examples of this are the full courtly description of the cock (81–98) and Chauntecleer's discussion of learned opinions about dreams (204–17). Chaucer enjoys both aspects: the high language and the elegant discussion of intellectual ideas on one side (they give him an opportunity to show off his skill and knowledge), and the comic deflation of farmyard events and bodily functions on the other (they provide the reward of laughter). Chaucer enriches his mock-heroic style by mixing in two other genres: the beast-fable and the exemplary story (sometimes called the *exemplum*). Both these genres traditionally involve moral teaching (think of Aesop's fables, or Beatrix Potter's), but Chaucer uses the comic effect of describing farmyard events in the epic style to provoke laughter at (and thus to undermine) the moral tendencies of both genres. (See Interpretations, pp. 91–7.) The key to reading *The Nun's Priest's Tale* is to remember that however complex the language and however specialized the ideas, Chaucer is trying to make us laugh. Modern intellectual comedies such as *Monty Python's Flying Circus* aim at a similar effect.

Another topic which pervades the tale is rhetoric. Rhetoric was a training in the use of language which was formulated in Ancient Greece and Rome and which was widely taught throughout Europe until the eighteenth century. It aimed to make people into better debaters and writers by teaching them how to devise material, how to organize a speech, and how to write in a style that was clear, persuasive and impressive. In the Middle Ages several authors produced handbooks of rhetoric adapted to the demands of writing poetry, among them Geoffrey de Vinsauf, whose Latin verse work *Poetria nova* (New Poetry), composed around 1200, Chaucer refers to in *The Nun's Priest's Tale* (581). Geoffrey de Vinsauf was mainly concerned with stylistic devices (such as repetition, metaphor, and simile) and with techniques for amplification (making your subject seem more important to your audience). Later Notes will point out passages in which particular techniques are employed. In this poem Chaucer uses many of the devices of rhetoric in a quite self-conscious way, as if he wants us to realize that he is writing in an elevated style appropriate to his 'heroic' subject-matter (and therefore funny as mock-heroic). But rhetoric taught the low style as well as the heroic. We shall need to watch out for Chaucer's alternation between different levels of style. (See Interpretations, pp. 106–10.)

Within the tale Chaucer employs both a variety of narrators and a quantity of ironic narratorial comment. A simple example would be Chauntecleer's interruption to his first story (284–91). As the story reaches its climax and the corpse is discovered in the dungcart, Chauntecleer launches into an elaborate and over-the-top exclamation about murder always being discovered. This is funny because of its inappropriateness. In the second half of the tale The Nun's Priest makes many similar interjections into his tale (for example, 460–86, 572–608), which are enjoyable and funny. When this happens we may need to ask whether The Nun's Priest is the object of Chaucer's irony (in that Chaucer keeps having The Nun's Priest make inappropriate comments) or the creator of the irony (in that he is deliberately telling his story in an excessive and humorous manner). Sometimes it can be hard to decide between these alternatives. At other times Chaucer draws attention to the fact that the tale has several narrators (490–500): Chaucer, The Nun's Priest, Chauntecleer. And these storytellers also quote remarks made by other authors (such as Cato and St Paul). As we read, we shall often have to think carefully about who is speaking and with what degree of irony. (See Interpretations, pp. 102–6.)

A description of the poor widow: lines 55–80

The Tale begins with a detailed and realistic description of the widow who owns Chauntecleer and the hens. She lives at the margin of a village, up against the wood (57). Her poverty is expressed in her small cottage and her meagre diet (56, 67–70, 76–9). But her diet makes her healthy (71–3), and her poverty breeds a philosophical attitude for which The Nun's Priest praises her (60, 73–5). (See Interpretations, pp. 100–2.) The association of poverty and virtue is found elsewhere in *The Canterbury Tales* (for example in *The Clerk's Tale* and the *General Prologue*) and in *Piers Plowman*, written by Chaucer's contemporary William Langland.

Her landholding is small and her animals few, so, like other poor English peasants, she supplements her own farming activities by working as a dairywoman (*deye* [80]) for the lord of the manor. The extreme realism of this description and the widow's humility provide a frame for (and a contrast to) the unlikely courtliness of the goings-on in her farmyard. But the description also invokes contrasts with other, more extravagant ways of life, for example when her sleeping-room is called a bower (*bour* [66]), or in the references to the richer diet she does not enjoy (68–9, 71, 76). In the *General Prologue* several of the pilgrims are characterized through eating and diet, among them two whom The Nun's Priest might have reason to refer to: The Monk, who told the previous tale, and The Nun's Priest's employer, The Prioress. (See Appendix, p. 159 and compare with the *General Prologue*, lines 118–207.)

55 **somdeel stape in age** somewhat advanced in age.

56 **whilom** once (a traditional word to use at the beginning of a story).

narwe narrow, small.

57 **grove** copse, small wood.

dale valley.

59 **thilke** the same, that. Since the day that her husband died.

60 Patience (*pacience*) or uncomplaining endurance was considered a virtuous response to misfortune.

61 For her property (*catel*) and her income (*rente*) were small.

62–3 By careful management (*housbondrie*) of what God gave her, she provided (*foond*) for herself and also her two daughters.

64 **and namo** and no more (a formulaic phrase used to provide a rhyme).

65 **keen** cows.

that highte Malle who was called Molly.

66 Many small dwellings had a central hearth with no chimney (hence the soot). The hall was the main room of a house, the bower a side room for sleeping. Some critics regard these as grand words to apply to the widow's cottage, and find ironic humour in this passage.

68 **poynaunt** sharp, spicy.

never a deel none at all.

69 **deyntee** choice, delicious. Compare with the description of The Prioress, *General Prologue*, 128–31. (See Appendix, p. 159 and Interpretations, p. 102.)

70 **accordant to hir cote** in keeping with her house.

71 **Repleccioun** over-eating.

72 **Attempree** moderate.

phisik medicine. Medieval authorities argued that moderate eating and simple food were the best way to remain healthy.

73 **hertes suffisaunce** contentment of heart.

74 **lette** prevent. The implication is that the widow did not suffer at all from gout, which can be caused by eating too much meat.

75 Apoplexy is an illness, sudden in its onset (hence 'apopleptic fit'), which paralyses the brain and the muscles. It is caused by a rush of blood to the head. In the medieval view an excess of blood might be caused by an unbalanced or excessive diet.

77 **bord**   table. How does the contrast of colours in these two lines bring out the character of the widow?

78 **foond**   found.

79 Grilled bacon and sometimes an egg or two. Compare the widow's diet with that of The Prioress's dogs, in the *General Prologue*, 147. (See Appendix, p. 159.)

80 **maner deye**   sort of dairywoman (responsible for the milking, cheese and butter making, and the poultry of the nearby manor, the chief house of the village, belonging to its feudal lord).

A description of Chauntecleer: lines 81–98

The hero of the tale, the widow's cockerel, is introduced with a description which follows the instructions of rhetoric. The description begins with comparisons which raise Chauntecleer above the ordinary. First, he is better at crowing than other cockerels, and more tuneful than a church organ (86–8). Then he is a better time-keeper than the abbey clock, with an innate understanding of planetary motion (89–92). Finally, each of his parts is described and compared with valuable courtly objects (93–8). Comparison and description were both aspects of amplification, the part of rhetoric which aimed to make things seem more impressive. (See Notes, pp. 37–9 and Interpretations, pp. 92, 100–2, 106-10.) What is the effect of describing a cockerel in such an elaborate way?

81–2 Presumably the yard has a wooden fence (or a hedge [452]) to keep out predators and a ditch outside (*withoute*) to drain away rainwater.

83 Chauntecleer is the name of the cock in the *Roman de Renart*, one of Chaucer's sources for *The Nun's Priest's Tale*. (See Notes, p. 63.) The name emphasizes his clear singing.

84 **nas his peer**   there was no equal to him.

85 **murie**   musical, tuneful. The next line shows that *orgon* must be plural (organs).

86   That play in the church on feast days.
87   **sikerer**   more reliable (more accurate?).
     logge   lodging (Chauntecleer's perch was inside the cottage [118]).
88   **orlogge**   clock. Perhaps an abbey *orlogge* was more elaborate than an ordinary *clokke*, but few households would have had clocks. Organs and clocks were among the most complex machines medieval craftsmen produced. What would be the point of saying that Chauntecleer performed his functions better than either of them?
89–92   This passage depends on the belief, widespread in the Middle Ages, that a cock would crow every hour. The Nun's Priest describes Chauntecleer's ability to crow at the right time, using the technical language of astronomy. The equinoctial (*equynoxial*) is an imaginary line across the sky corresponding to the position of the equator. This line is circular and the rotation of the earth (which medieval people regarded as a rotation of the sky) means that every part of the line is theoretically visible in each 24-hour day; hence every 15 degree sector of the equinoctial corresponds to one hour (91). The ascension (*ascencioun*) is the point where this line crosses the horizon. Chauntecleer is said to know by instinct both where the ascension is (for his town, since this point and the arc of the equinoctial line would vary according to latitude) and when fifteen degrees of the equinoctial have passed over the horizon. This enables him to crow accurately on every hour.
92   **amended**   bettered.
93   The comb (*coomb*) is the crest on the cock's head. The coral Chaucer knew came from the Red Sea and the Mediterranean and was red. Throughout the description Chauntecleer's colours are compared with courtly or valuable things.
94   **batailled**   crenellated, in the shape of battlements.
95   **byle**   bill.
     jeet   jet.
96   **asure**   lapis lazuli (a blue stone). Azure is also the word for blue in heraldry, the art of describing and regulating coats of arms.
     toon   toes.
98   **burned**   burnished. What impression of the cock do all these splendid colours give you?

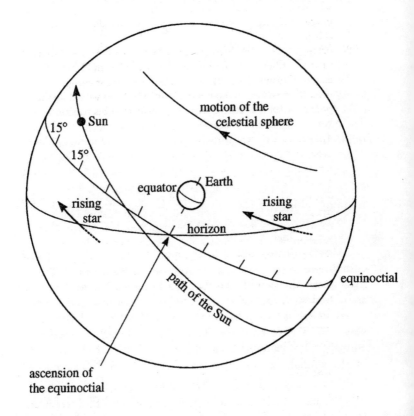

This diagram illustrates lines 89–92. We are looking at the universe from the outside. The stars and planets are imagined to be on a hollow sphere ('the celestial sphere') with the Earth at its centre. The celestial sphere rotates once every 24 hours (remember that medieval people thought the stars and planets moved around the Earth).

Chauntecleer's hens: lines 99–115

Like other cocks Chauntecleer has several hens to service, in his case seven, but as a noble creature his love is given particularly to Lady Pertelote, who is described in the same way as the heroine in a romance. She is beautiful, courteous, modest, companionable (103–6), and has complete control of his heart (108–9). It is a joy to hear them sing love songs together. So far The Nun's Priest plays with the contrast between the language of noble love and the situation of the farmyard. But what is the effect of his explanation: 'at that time, I am told, birds and animals could speak and sing' (114–15)? Perhaps The Nun's Priest is naively justifying his story, or perhaps he (or Chaucer standing behind him) is pointing up the absurdity of the genre of the beast-fable (which is so familiar to us as readers that we accept it unquestioningly).

Most cultures tell stories about animals. They usually combine humour with commonsense teaching about how to manage in the world. In the West many animal fables are associated with the name of Aesop, a slave who lived on the Greek island of Samos in the sixth century BC, though the written versions we have are later. Beast-fables depend on treating the animals as humans, and on assumptions about the characteristics of the animals (for example that a fox is crafty, that a cockerel is proud). They convey commonplace moral teaching in a humorous way. Most beast-fables take the form for granted; Chaucer's poem (either seriously or for humorous purposes) questions the basis of the genre. (See Interpretations, pp. 91–7.)

99 *Gentil* is a key word of medieval courtly culture, principally meaning 'of high birth', but conveying values of sensitivity, courtesy, and moral virtue. What is the effect of applying this word to a cock?

100 Where the previous line emphasized courtly and political values, this one points to physical realities (seven hens to serve

his pleasure [*plesaunce*]). What part does the rhyme play in linking these contrasting ideas?

101 What is the effect of sisters (*sustres*) and mistresses (*paramours*)? Are any of these value-laden human categories applicable in the farmyard? Some critics think the joke is made even better by the allusion to 'my sister, my spouse' in The Song of Solomon (a book of the Bible), chapter 4, verses 9–12, where the 'beloved' is interpreted as the church, thus allowing her to be both sister and spouse to Christ.

103 **hewed** coloured.

104 **cleped** called.
   Faire beautiful. *Damoysele* usually means a young unmarried lady of noble birth. Pertelote is a name invented by Chaucer (the *Roman de Renart* had Pinte as the name of Chauntecleer's beloved), which R. A. Pratt (*Speculum*, 47, p. 655) interprets as 'someone who destroys one's fate', because *perte* is connected with loss or destruction, and *lot* with fate. Compare with Note to line 398, p. 61.

105 **discreet** wise, kind.
   debonaire gracious, modest. (See Interpretations, pp. 114–7).

106 And friendly, and conducted herself so well (beautifully, graciously).

107 Among all the courtly words Chaucer delicately reminds us of the life-cycle of the chicken.

108 **in hoold** in keeping, in possession. Compare (and contrast) with Note to line 99 above.

109 **loken... lith** bound fast (by love) in every limb.

110 **wel... therwith** he was happy at it (see A Note on Chaucer's English, p. 139.)

112 **gan to sprynge** rose. In Middle English the verb 'spring' had many meanings connected with 'begin'; its Modern English equivalents are more specific (such as 'sprout', 'blossom', 'grow').

113 **accord** harmony. 'My Love has gone away' was the first line (and title) of a popular song. There may be a joke in singing together a song about lovers being apart, but lovers are often happy to sing sad love songs.

115 **koude** knew how to. (See Notes, p. 44.)

Chauntecleer's dream: lines 116–41

One dawn Chauntecleer groaned in his sleep, because he had a nightmare about a strange, frightening animal, like a dog but red and gold in colour. We learn a great deal about different medieval attitudes to dreams in the debate between Chauntecleer and Pertelote which follows. Evidently, Chauntecleer has never seen a fox, but his reaction accords with the medieval belief that animals have a fear of their predators which is instinctive rather than learned by experience. What can we learn about the relationship between Chauntecleer and Pertelote from their exchange here (119–29)?

116 **bifel** it happened.
  dawenynge dawn. Many philosophers believed dawn dreams to be prophetic. (See Notes, pp. 47, 52.)
121 Like one who is severely (*soore*) troubled (*drecched*) in his dream.
122 **roore** roar.
123 **agast** afraid.
124 **eyleth** troubles, afflicts.
125 **verray** fine. How do you understand Pertelote's tone here?
127 **take... agrief** do not be upset.
128 **me mette** I dreamed (the impersonal verb, see A Note on Chaucer's English, p. 139).
  meschief trouble, misfortune.
129 **afright** frightened.
130 **swevene** dream.
  recche aright interpret favourably.
131 **prisoun** captivity.
132–9 Chauntecleer's dream is an accurate prophecy of the fox and his intentions, though not of the whole course of the tale. This casts doubt on Pertelote's theory on dreams (see lines 156–9 and Notes, p. 49), but also makes Chauntecleer more culpable for ignoring the warning. In the *Roman de Renart*, the cock dreams of having a red fur coat with a bone collar forced on him, which leaves a little more room for differences of interpretation.

134 **hound**   dog.
   wolde han maad areest   intended to seize.
136 **bitwixe**   between.
139 **smal**   slim.
140 **Yet**   still.

Pertelote responds to Chauntecleer's dream: lines 142–203

Pertelote is dismayed by Chauntecleer's fear. She tells him how far his cowardice makes him fall short of an ideal husband (144–54). No one should be afraid of dreams because dreams are only the result of an excess of humours (157). She prescribes a herbal laxative to reduce the humour of choler in her 'husband'. Do you see Pertelote here as practical and helpful or as dismissive of Chauntecleer? Do these remarks reveal Pertelote's character or should we see them as anti-female satire (mocking comments alleged to be typical of married women)?

The view of dreams which Pertelote develops here (like Chauntecleer's later view) is somewhat one-sided. Classical and medieval writers generally accepted that some dreams were prophetic, while others could be the result of worry or of an imbalance of humours. What Pertelote says of all dreams, medieval writers would say only of one particular type, the *somnium naturale*, the dream whose causes are purely physiological. (See Interpretations, pp. 110–4.)

Pertelote's account rests on the theory of humours, a staple of classical and medieval medicine, which held that the body contained four fluids or humours (blood, phlegm, red or yellow bile – also called choler – and black bile – also called melancholy). The excess of one of these humours could lead to disease. The humours in the body would fluctuate according to diet, the seasons, astrological influences, and the state of particular internal organs. If a humour was present in excess a doctor might employ blood-letting, leeches, or (as Pertelote suggests here) purgatives in the attempt to reduce the humour in excess and restore a healthy balance. The humours also played a role in determining character (189). The long-term preponderance of one of them would predispose a person to be, for example, phlegmatic or melancholic. Notice that we still use the vocabulary of the humours in discussing character. More information on the theory of humours and on its relation to dreams can be found in W. C. Curry, *Chaucer and the Medieval Sciences*, pp. 10–19, 205–8. (See Interpretations, pp. 112–3.)

Pertelote uses the detail of Chauntecleer's dream to make her analysis. The red-yellow colour of the dream animal's skin indicates an excess of choler (or yellow bile), the black tips show an excess of melancholy (or black bile). This is thorough and logical, but the fact that we recognize the dream animal as a fox renders comic her elaborate interpretation. Chaucer is exploiting the resourcefulness of medieval science as much as he can, but twisting it in the direction of comedy.

142 *Avoy* is clearly an exclamation but there is no agreement about what it means. Equivalents proposed include: away, alas, come, and shame.

hertelees coward.

146 **what so** whatever.

148 **hardy** bold.

free generous, noble. The qualities Pertelote lists as desirable in a husband are almost exactly those which the wife in *The Shipman's Tale* says all women look for:

> Hardy and wise, and riche, and therto free
> And buxom unto his wyf and fressh abedde   (176–7)

and reflect other medieval discussions of the ideal husband. Perhaps this helps us see Pertelote as an example of a medieval woman, rather than just a hen. There may also be ironies in Pertelote's list. *Free* denotes the qualities suited to a free man, whereas Chauntecleer is an owned animal. Pertelote omits *and fressh abedde* (a quality which Chauntecleer certainly does not lack) from the list above.

149 **secree** discreet, able to keep secrets. Strictly speaking this was a quality more important in a lover (who was expected never to reveal his love to others) than in a husband.

nygard miser.

150 **tool** weapon.

151 **avantour** boaster. Men who boasted of their conquests were a threat to the reputations of medieval women.

154 Pertelote is attacking Chauntecleer's honour, claiming that he has the outward shape of a man (the beard) but lacks the inner substance (bravery). Again the specific human reference reminds us of the running joke that both these creatures are birds and that the standards by which she is condemning him are inappropriate and absurd. But the joke has a further turn because cocks have a twist of feathers at the neck which some people call a 'beard'.

vanitee emptiness.

157 Dreams are caused (*engendren*) by excesses (of humours – see Notes, pp. 47–8).

158 **fume** exhalations, vapours (gases given off by the humours, which trouble the brain).

complecciouns temperaments (the blending of the humours which together form each person's character and attitude).

161 **superfluytee** superfluity, excess.

162 Choler (*colera*), one of the four humours of the body, could be yellow or red. Here Pertelote associates its red aspect with the red details from Chauntecleer's dream.

163 **dreden** fear.

164 **arwes** arrows. Perhaps medieval arrows were red, perhaps the arrows in question were fiery, or perhaps arrows are associated with *contek* (166).

lemes flames.

166 **contek** strife (associated with red because of bloodshed).

whelpes dogs (which may have been red?).

167 **malencolie** melancholy (see Notes, pp. 47–8).

169 **boles blake** black bulls.

170 This line slightly interrupts the construction of the sentence: Or else (because they fear that) black devils will take them.

172 That cause great distress to people in their sleep.

173 **lightly** quickly.

174 Cato (*Catoun*) here refers to the book of short proverbs, *Disticha Catonis*, which was used in medieval schools as the most elementary Latin reader. No doubt the book derived some of its prestige from a supposed link with the Roman Cato the elder (234–149 BC), famous for the pithy expression of traditional moral values, though it was actually composed in the fourth century AD.

175 **Ne... dremes**   Pay no attention to dreams. The two negatives do not cancel each other (see A Note on Chaucer's English, p. 139). This phrase translates the Latin words found in *Disticha Catonis*: '*Somnia ne cures*' ('Do not trust in dreams').

176 **flee**   fly. Presumably their perch (118) is among the beams (*bemes*) of the hall.

177 **as taak**   take (a polite form of command).
Laxatyf   laxative. Pertelote's idea is that Chauntecleer should purge the humour which is in excess and which has given him the bad dream.

179 **conseille**   advise.

181 **for**   so that.

182 Normally one would go to a pharmacist (*apothecarie*) for a herbal cure, but since there is none nearby, and since she is wise, Pertelote will prescribe her own herbs. Her friendly practicality is enhanced by the absurd idea of the chicken going to the chemist.

184 **hele**   good health.
prow   profit, benefit.

185 **tho**   those.

186–7 Which have among their qualities naturally (the ability) to purge you above and below (that is, to make you vomit and defecate).

189 Pertelote is saying that Chauntecleer's temperament (*compleccioun*) is choleric. His character is dominated by a life-long preponderance of choler. On the medieval view this makes him liable to be hot-tempered. Pertelote wants him to avoid anything which will increase his already high choler into the excess which would cause bad dreams and disease. But surely there is also a joke here. Since the ascension is the part of the sky rising over the horizon (see Note to line 89, p. 42) Pertelote

must be suggesting that Chauntecleer should avoid sunrise, which would be hard for a cockerel.

190 **Ware** beware. When the sun is at its most powerful (from the astrological point of view) it will increase the hot humours in the body (choler and blood). These times will be especially dangerous to Chauntecleer if he is already full (*repleet* [191]) of choler, because of what he has eaten or for other reasons. (See Notes, p. 47–8.)

192 **leye** lay, bet.
grote groat (obsolete fourpenny coin). A groat was a worthwhile, but not a large sum of money. In London in 1378 you could buy ten eggs for a penny or a roast hen for fourpence (E. Rickert (ed.) *Chaucer's World*, pp. 30–31).

193 **fevere terciane** tertian fever (a fever which becomes stronger every other day). Some writers associate tertian fever especially with choler.

194 **agu** ague, acute fever.
bane death.

195 A digestive (a medicine to promote the digestion of food) would normally be taken before a course of laxatives, as Pertelote suggests. Worms are included in some recipes for digestives but they are also part of a chicken's natural diet.

197–200 Medieval authorities classify all the herbs Pertelote lists as laxatives, but some of them are very strong. We would call them (in order): spurge laurel, lesser centaury, fumitory, black hellebore, caper spurge (*katapuce*), (?) buckthorn berries, (?) buckthorn. Does the long list of herbs increase our respect for Petelote's knowledge or is the effect comic?

200 **ther mery is** where it is pleasant (the expression is forced by the rhyme).

202 **myrie** merry.
fader kyn father's family. The fox later appeals to Chauntecleer's pride in his family (529–55).

203 Pertelote ends her speech with reassurance but she began by attacking Chauntecleer for cowardice (142–54). Over the whole speech do you think she is supporting him or belittling him?

Chauntecleer begins his reply: lines 204–17

Chauntecleer thanks Pertelote for her display of learning (*loore*), but argues against her conclusions. He first takes up the authority she has cited (174), arguing that the opinions of wiser men must be set against Cato's view, and that in fact dreams are prophetic. What sense of Chauntecleer's character do you get from this passage?

Whereas Pertelote says that dreams are caused by an excess of humours, and Chauntecleer claims that dreams are prophetic, most medieval authorities would say that dreams may fall into either category. Chauntecleer later allows that many a dream (that is, not all) should be feared (343). R. A. Pratt has shown (*Speculum*, 52) that much of what both chickens say about dreams is taken from a commentary on the Book of Wisdom (an apocryphal book of the Bible, see Note to line 35, p. 34) by Robert Holkot (died 1349). The significance of dreams was a much debated topic in the Middle Ages and Chaucer used other sources as well. (See Interpretations, pp. 110–4.)

204 **graunt mercy** many thanks. Do you take this as genuine or ironic?
205 **daun** master (envisaged here as an academic title perhaps).
207 Although he said that dreams were not to be feared.
209 **auctorite** authority. One of the most common ways of arguing in the Middle Ages was to pit the views of one author against another. More reliable or more famous authors weighed more heavily.
210 **so moot I thee** as I may prosper (a common, fairly mild exclamation).
211 **sentence** meaning, opinion.
213 **significaciouns** indications, signs.
214 **tribulaciouns** troubles.
216–17 There is no need to argue in support of this, the true test (of experience, presumably) shows it in practice. Chauntecleer

offers this remark as a transition from his opening point
(contesting the validity of Cato's opinion by contrasting it
with other unnamed authorities) to his stories (or *exempla*, see
Notes, p. 54) which involve dreams which were significant.
The dividing line between authority and experience is rather
blurred, though, since Chauntecleer's stories are taken from
authors.

Chauntecleer's first story: lines 218–96

Chauntecleer tells of two travellers who were forced to lodge
separately in a strange town. One of them dreamed that the other
was calling out to him in his sleep. He ignored the dream twice,
so the third time his friend appeared to him to say that he had
been murdered and that his body would be found hidden in a
cart of dung at the west gate of the town. When his friend could
not be found in the morning, the traveller went to the west gate,
where he found the cart, had it emptied, and discovered the
body. Under torture the wicked innkeeper and the cart-driver
confessed to the crime. Do you find the story entertaining? Or is
the teaching the most important thing about it?

A much briefer version of the story than Chaucer's was told
by the famous Roman orator and philosopher Cicero (106–43 BC)
in *De divinatione* (On Divination), a book about fate and the
possibility of predicting events. Cicero's version of the story was
adapted by Valerius Maximus, a Roman historian of the first
century AD, for his book of moral stories. This version appears
verbatim in the commentary on the Book of Wisdom by Robert
Holkot (see Notes, p. 52), which we know Chaucer used in
composing *The Nun's Priest's Tale*. The story was retold by the
thirteenth-century German philosopher Albertus Magnus, in his
treatise on dreams. R. A. Pratt (*Speculum*, 52) has shown that
Chaucer takes over elements from all three versions before him.
(Chaucer does not appear to have used Valerius Maximus
directly.)

You may find it interesting to compare Chaucer's much longer version of the story to Cicero's. (See Appendix, p. 159.) In making his adaptation Chaucer adds speeches which dramatize the characters' emotions, narratorial comments which point up the moral, and details of medieval life which add vividness to the story. Do the additions tell us about Chaucer's way of telling stories or about Chauntecleer's character?

R. A. Pratt claims that the overall tendency of Chaucer's adaptation is to emphasize the horror of the murder and the folly of taking a sceptical position about dreams. Does this correspond to your reading of the story (and its source)? If Pratt is right we can see how both emphases suit Chauntecleer's purposes in telling the tale, namely to insist on the justice of his own fear, and to reject Pertelote's scepticism. We would expect Chauntecleer to emphasize the aspects of the story which support his case, but if the story reflects his interests too strongly his audience may question the truth of what he says. *The Nun's Priest's Tale* raises within itself issues about the relationship between a story and its teller which pervade *The Canterbury Tales* as a whole.

This story and the next one Chauntecleer tells would both be classified by medieval writers as *exempla* (Latin for 'examples'), that is to say stories which illustrate a moral point. As a matter of fact all the stories in Valerius Maximus' book, *Facta et Dicta Memorabilia* (Deeds and Words Worth Remembering), fall into this category. *Exempla* are stories which depend on a tight relationship between a story and its moral. Later in *The Nun's Priest's Tale* we shall be asked to question whether the apparent morals of the tale really apply.

218 **rede** read. Critics have argued for either Valerius Maximus or Cicero as 'one of the greatest authors' on the basis of the sources (see Notes, p. 53), but the point may be comic. Chauntecleer is opposing Cato with an author so great that he cannot remember his name.

220 **entente** intention, purpose.

221 **happed**   it happened.

222 **congregacioun**   gathering, crowd.

223 **streit of herbergage**   shortage of accommodation.

224 **o**   one.

225 **ylogged**   lodged.

227 **departen**   part.

228 **hostelrye**   lodging.

229 **as it wolde falle**   as it chanced. References to fortune are
frequent in this passage (221, 226, 233–4). Perhaps we should
connect this with Chauntecleer's outlook on life or with the
discussion of free will outlined in the Notes, p. 67.

230 What would be the effect of taking this as an allusion to the
nativity of Jesus?

231 If the stall is far down the yard the man's cries will not be
heard in the street.

233 **aventure**   chance, lot.

236 **ther**   where.

237 **gan... calle**   called (see A Note on Chaucer's English, p. 139).

242 **abrayde**   started, woke suddenly.

244 **took... keep**   took no notice of it.

245 Notice how in Chauntecleer's story the traveller (wrongly)
calls a dream empty (*vanitee*) just as Pertelote had (156).

248 **slawe**   slain.

250 **morwe tyde**   morning time.

252 **shaltow**   (=*shalt thow*) you shall. Without sewers, dung carts
were required to clean the town and provide manure to the
surrounding fields.

253 **prively**   secretly.

254 Have that cart seized immediately.

255 **sooth**   truth. Here he gives a motive for the murder, where
before the outcome has been blamed on fortune.

256 **point**   detail.

257 **pitous**   piteous, sad.
hewe   colour.

260 **in**   inn, lodging.

264–5 **Sire... toun**   Sir, your friend has gone. He left town at
daybreak.

266 **gan... suspecioun**   became suspicious.

268 **lette**   delay.

270 **wente... lond** gone as if to manure the land.
271 **arrayed** arranged, disposed.
    wise manner, way.
272 **devyse** describe. What is the effect of mentioning the audience (*ye*) here?
273 **with... herte** boldly.
276 **lith gapyng upright** lies facing upwards with mouth wide open.
277–8 I appeal to the magistrates who should protect and govern this city.
279 *Harrow* and *Allas* are both cries of distress.
281 **out sterte** leaped up, rushed into action.
283 **al newe** very recently.
284–91 Chauntecleer interrupts his story, with an apostrophe ('O God...'), a direct address to God to indicate the strength of emotion he feels. This is a standard rhetorical device. Students of rhetoric were instructed to prepare highly-wrought paragraphs on general moral themes which one might frequently have cause to use. Chauntecleer's words here are just such a moral commonplace. (See Interpretations, p. 110.)
285 **biwreyest** reveal.
287 **wlatsom and abhomynable** revolting and hateful.
289 **heled** concealed.
291 'Murder will out' is a proverb which also occurs in *The Prioress's Tale* (576).
293 **hent** seized. *Pyned* (293) and *engyned* (294) mean tortured and racked, a normal part of judicial investigations in the Middle Ages.
295 **biknewe** acknowledged, confessed.

Chauntecleer's second story: lines 297–343

In Chauntecleer's second story, two travellers are held up in port for a long time by a contrary wind. Just when the wind changes one of them has a dream which prophesies drowning. Consequently, he refuses to embark in the morning. His friend mocks his superstition, takes ship and is drowned. Versions of this tale were available to Chaucer from Cicero's *De divinatione* and from the commentary of Holkot, who followed Valerius Maximus very closely (see Notes, p. 53). Chaucer used both versions and expanded them considerably. He added the words spoken in the dream, the speech of the sceptical friend and many incidental details which ground the story in medieval life. What does this second story add to its predecessor? Why does Chauntecleer include both?

297 **been to drede**   ought to be feared. Chauntecleer uses this expression to conclude both stories (compare with line 343).

298–9 Both stories are in Cicero and Holkot, adjacent in Cicero, farther apart in Holkot; in the opposite order to Chaucer in both his sources. When Chaucer states that the second story is in the next chapter of the same book, he may be being forgetful or disguising his source.

300 I do not lie, as I may have joy or happiness.

304 **tarie**   delay, wait.

305 **myrie... syde**   pleasantly situated beside a harbour.

306 **agayn**   towards.

307 **hem leste**   it pleased them, they wanted.

309 **casten hem**   planned.

310 But listen. A great wonder befell that same man.

312 He dreamed a strange dream just before dawn. (Compare with line 116.)

314 **abyde**   remain.

315 **wende**   go, leave.

316 **dreynt**   drowned.

318 **his... lette**   to delay his journey.

321 **scorned... faste**   poured scorn on him.

324 I consider your dreams worthless (I do not value your dreams at one straw).

325 **japes**   deceptions, tricks. (Compare with line 245.)

326 **alday**   continually. Owls were birds of ill omen. In some English manuscript illustrations apes and owls are linked as representatives of evil. The speaker intends the pairing as an example of the absurdity of dreams, but the outcome of the story shows how little he understands.

327 **maze** delusion, source of bewilderment. How does the friend convey his contempt for those who believe in dreams? Does this help Chauntecleer attack Pertelote's view, or do we conclude that both views of dreams can be criticized forcefully?

330 And so perversely (*wilfully*) waste your time (*tyde*) through sloth.

331 **it... day** it saddens me; and so farewell.

334 I know not why, nor what misfortune afflicted (*eyled*) it.

335 **casuelly** by chance. (Compare with line 229.) Perhaps the refusal to name a local cause leaves space for the operation of fate.

337 This line emphasizes the suddenness and randomness of the disaster.

340 **leere** learn.

341 **to recchelees** too heedless, careless.

Chauntecleer cites more examples and authorities: lines 344–90

In order to drive home his points that dreams sometimes foretell the future and that it is wise to be warned by them, Chauntecleer now summarizes a series of more or less well-known stories and cites further authorities. Two of the stories are from the Bible, and three from history: Andromache from medieval retellings of classical epic; Kenelm from the legends of the English saints, and Croesus probably from the *Roman de la Rose*. Chauntecleer also cites the authority of Macrobius, a scholar who lived around 400 AD, and who wrote a commentary on Cicero's *Somnium Scipionis* (Dream of Scipio). Macrobius's commentary included an elaborate classification of dreams and many explanations of points in astronomy and philosophy, which made it a prime source for Chaucer (especially in his early poem *The Parliament of Fowls*) and his contemporaries. It is fully described in C. S. Lewis's *The Discarded Image*. Chauntecleer's examples include the Bible, Christian and pagan history, and philosophy. It is a very impressive case for a cockerel to assemble.

344–6 Mercia (*Mercenrike*) was the Anglo-Saxon kingdom which
occupied areas of the English Midlands between about 500
AD and 870. St Kenelm is said to have succeeded to the throne
of Mercia in 821, at the age of seven, and shortly afterwards
to have been murdered on the instructions of his sister.
Legends concerning his life began to circulate in the late tenth
century and Chaucer may have read about him either in Latin
sources or in *The South English Legendary*, a verse collection of
saints' lives assembled in the thirteenth century.

348 *Avysioun* is a technical term for a prophetic dream.

    say saw.

349 **norice** nurse.

    expowned explained, interpreted.

351 **Fortraisoun** against treason.

    nas but was only.

352 **litel... toold** he attached little significance.

353 So has explanatory force here, like 'because'. Should we take
holy (*hooly*) as equivalent to 'innocent', if it makes him ignore
dreams?

354 **levere** rather. Is this mainly funny, in that Chauntecleer can
no more wear a shirt (*sherte*) than he can read a book, or is he
also alluding to Kenelm being murdered by his sister (since
Pertelote is Chauntecleer's sister [101] and he later suggests
that she wants to poison him [389])?

355 *Legende* is the usual word for the biography of a saint.

357 Macrobius was not the author of the *Dream of Scipio*, but he
wrote the commentary which preserved this work in the
Middle Ages and which Chaucer cites in lines 358–60. The
dream foretold that Scipio (*Cipioun* [358]) would destroy
Carthage. In fact the *Dream of Scipio* was not an independent
work but one of the surviving fragments of Cicero's *On the
Republic* (about 51 BC).

362 If Pertelote were to read the Old Testament book of Daniel,
as Chauntecleer suggests, she would find many examples of
dreams which come true (chapter 2, verses 31–46, and
chapters 4, 7–8 and 10).

364–9 Joseph has two prophetic dreams in Genesis, 37:5–10. He
successfully interprets the dreams of Pharaoh's baker and
butler in chapter 40, and of Pharaoh himself in chapter 41.

This last dream prophesied seven years of plenty followed by
seven years of famine.

365 **Wher** whether. What is the effect of expressing these ideas
(compare with lines 363 and 369) as indirect questions rather
than statements?

369 Whether they perceived in their dreams nothing which came
about (*noon effect*).

370 Whoever wants to search the histories (*actes*) of different
countries (*remes*).

372 **Lo** look, consider. Croesus was king of Lydia around
560–546 BC and was legendary for his wealth. Chaucer's story
of Croesus' dream and his death, which is told in full in *The
Monk's Tale*, immediately before The Knight interrupts,
comes not from the Greek historians but from a retelling of
the story in the thirteenth-century French work the *Roman de
la Rose*, parts of which Chaucer translated.

374 **anhanged** hanged.

375 The story of Andromache's dream is found in late classical
and medieval retellings of the story of Troy. Chaucer's
knowledge of these sources is shown by his use of them in
Troilus and Criseyde, his romance set in Troy.

376 **Ector** Hector, the best warrior on the Trojan side.
sholde lese was to lose.

380 **availle** be of use.

381 **natheles** nevertheless.

384 **ny** nigh, near.
dwelle remain, delay. Chauntecleer will have to go outside
to crow at daybreak.

385–96 See Interpretations, p. 100.

386 Perhaps Chauntecleer is stressing the truth of his dream by
calling it an *avisioun* (compare with line 348) but he has
already also called it a *swevene* (130), a more neutral word for
dream. (See Interpretations, pp. 110–4.)

387 **Adversitee** trouble.

388 **telle... no stoor** set no store, have no trust.

389 **venymes** poisons.

390 **I hem diffye** I reject them.

Chauntecleer is overcome by Pertelote's beauty: lines 391–420

After such a lengthy display of learning, the tale returns to the domestic life of the cockerel and his hens. Chauntecleer is so comforted by the sight and touch of Pertelote that he forgets his fearful dream. He flies out of the hall, finds a grain of corn, clucks for his hens and copulates with Pertelote. But he does not completely abandon learning. He says in Latin that woman is man's downfall, translating it in a completely different way for Pertelote's benefit. Are we to see this as typical of the way Chauntecleer uses his learning? Do you think The Nun's Priest is also getting at The Prioress, who may not know enough Latin to appreciate the insult (compare with the *General Prologue*, 124–6, see Appendix, p. 159)? Or might there also be, as some critics argue, a more serious point: woman is man's ruin because she is his joy and bliss? (See Interpretations, pp. 117–20.)

391 Now let us speak of something cheerful and stop all this.
392 **so… blis**   as I may have happiness.
393 God has shown me great favour in one thing.
395 Perhaps redness is a sign of beauty in Pertelote as it was in Chauntecleer (93) or perhaps it makes a special appeal to him because of his choleric temperament (162).
396 It causes all my fear to vanish (literally, die). (See Interpretations, p. 117–8.)
397 **In principio**   (Latin) In the beginning (the first words both of Genesis and John). The early verses of John were used for various religious purposes (including exorcism and healing) in the Middle Ages.
398 (Latin) Woman is man's ruin. The phrase is part of a diatribe against women found in various medieval Latin sources.
399 **sentence**   meaning.
400 **al his blis**   his entire happiness.
402 **Al be**   although.
   ryde   mount. Is Chauntecleer complimentary or manipulative here?

405 **diffye**   scorn, repudiate. Does this make Pertelote
Chauntecleer's ruin?

406–18 See Interpretations, pp. 94–5.

406 **fley**   flew. The hens follow in the next line.

408 **chuk**   cluck.

409 Medieval encyclopaedias of natural history report that when
the cock finds a grain of wheat he calls to his hens to share it.

410 **Real**   royal, regal. Because of his generosity and his
overcoming of fear?

411 **fethered**   clasped with his wings.

412 **trad**   trod, copulated with.
pryme   prime (9 a.m.). Compare the physicality of this line
with the courtliness of line 410. Does the sexual reference
suit The Nun's Priest's profession or his employer?

413 **grym leoun**   fierce lion. Should we see a connection between
Chauntecleer's sexual activity and his valour? Or is Chaucer
jokingly alternating warrior pride with farmyard reality?

416–8 The way these lines repeat the material of lines 408–10
suggests that Chaucer may have revised this passage, perhaps
to insert or delete material.

419 **in his pasture**   at his food, feeding.

420 The Nun's Priest announces that his story is about to begin.

Chauntecleer's precarious happiness: lines 421–48

The Nun's Priest makes a formal new beginning, grandly placing
his narrative in time and establishing Chauntecleer's mood.
Surrounded by his seven hens he observes the sun, the birds and
the flowers. But The Nun's Priest intervenes to warn him and
us that this joy will be short-lived. In many of his poems
Chaucer uses the technical language of astronomy, with its
cosmic overtones and the naming of the classical deities as
planets, as a grand-style way of establishing when events
occurred. In this case the effect is extended because his hero has
a natural facility for planetary measurement, learned cockerel
that he is. (See Interpretations, pp. 108–9.)

This passage also establishes the characteristic rhythm of the narrative part of the tale. Having announced that he will begin (420), The Nun's Priest writes a high-style opening, begins the story and then immediately interrupts it with a commentary. He seems to be teasing his audience by appearing to begin the story only to put it off again. But the commentary predicts the outcome of the story at the same time as postponing its opening. There is far more commentary and elaboration than story in *The Nun's Priest's Tale*, and we shall have to attend carefully to the games The Nun's Priest plays with his audience and his narrative. (See Interpretations, p. 96.)

Chaucer has two main sources for the story of the cock and the fox: a version of the fable told by Marie de France and an episode from the *Roman de Renart*. Marie's short fable provides the story of the flattering fox who captures the cock, but who is in turn tricked into opening his mouth. The *Roman de Renart* adds details about the farmyard, the name of Chauntecleer, his wife (named Pinte), and a dream. You will be able to see more about what Chaucer has added to his source by comparing *The Nun's Priest's Tale* with the summary of the episode from *Renart* provided in the Appendix (p. 159).

421 Medieval writers worked out from the Creation story that the world was created at the spring equinox (which fell around 12 March in the fourteenth century).

421–4 This is a grand way of saying 'on 3 May'. The grandeur comes partly from using many words where few would be sufficient, and partly from connecting the date with the Creation. This date is also important in *Troilus and Criseyde* and *The Knight's Tale*.

425 **Bifel** it happened.

428–9 Medieval astronomers (like modern astrologers) divided the sky into 12 sectors (of 30 degrees each) which were given names corresponding to the position of the stars in each sector. These are the signs of the zodiac. They offer a way of describing the position of the planets and, with reference to the position of the sun, the passing of the year. The sun would normally have entered the sign of Taurus on 11 April (remember that this is before the reform of the calendar; the modern dates are about ten days later), and so would have passed through 21 of its 30 degrees by 2 May. A little more (429) takes it to 3 May. J. D. North (*Review of English Studies*, 20, pp. 418–22) has calculated that the date for *The Nun's Priest's Tale* must be 3 May 1392, because that is the only Friday 3 May between 1382 and 1400 in which the sun had in fact passed 21 degrees of Taurus.

428 **yronne** run.

430 Chauntecleer knows the time by nature (*kynde*) and not by learning (*loore*), but Chaucer improves the joke by having him explain exactly how high the sun had got (433). (Compare with lines 87–91.)

431 **stevene** voice.

433 Forty-one degrees refers to the sun's elevation in the sky at 9 a.m. that day, not to its annual passage across the zodiac mentioned in line 429. Apparently Chauntecleer's measurements are correct.

435 We often read in Chaucer (and other medieval books) of nobles going out into the fields to pay their observances to May. The phrase indicates an almost religious admiration for the beauty of the spring. We must imagine that the chickens are doing the same. Just like humans they attribute happiness to birds!

436 **fresshe** new, young, blooming.
     sprynge grow.

437 **revel** pleasure.

438–48 The Nun's Priest breaks in with foreboding, quoting a proverb (happiness always ends in sorrow [439]). He then suggests that this proverb would make a fine moral for a historian of rhetorical bent (like Valerius Maximus?), and protests (ironically?) the truth of the story (445–7). All these comments raise the issue of the significance of the tale to the audience. Is it the prelude to a tragedy, the illustration of a well-worn moral, or is it untrue?

438 **sorweful cas** sad misfortune.

439 This phrase ultimately derives from Proverbs 14:13. It was taken up by Innocent III, who was Pope from 1198 to 1216, in

his *On Contempt for the World*. Chaucer translates the phrase
in a slightly different way in *The Man of Law's Tale* (424) and
Troilus and Criseyde (IV, 836): *The ende of blisse ay sorwe it
occupieth.*

440 **ago**   gone.

441–3 And if a master of rhetoric knew how to write beautifully he
might safely include this in a history (*cronycle* [442]) as a chief
(*sovereyn* [443]) point to notice (*notabilitee* [443]). Is this an
ironic undercutting of the moral (in that it overstates the
obvious) or is The Nun's Priest referring humorously to his
own tale?

444 **herkne**   listen to. How do you take this line?

445–7 The French prose romance *Lancelot* (composed around
1215–1230) was circulated widely in England and France in
the fourteenth century. In it Lancelot appears as the
paramount hero of the Round Table, noted especially for his
fidelity and ardour in love (hence line 447). Some romances
claimed that they were true in order to enhance their moral
value. The Nun's Priest may be mocking this type of claim
(since his story is as true as theirs, theirs must be untrue) or
he may be claiming that his beast-fable has as much validity in
its teaching as the higher genre of courtly romance. There
may also be an implication that the moral stories which men
attend to (444) are no more or less true than the romances
which women believe (447).

447 *That* may mean 'whom', referring to the man rather than the
romance.

448 **sentence**   subject-matter. (Compare with lines 420, 485.)

The fox lies in wait for Chauntecleer: lines 449–63

A fox who has been living in the nearby wood for three years has
broken into the farmyard and is lying low in a cabbage patch,
waiting for a chance to pounce on Chauntecleer. Employing the
rhetorical figure of apostrophe (see Note to line 284, p. 56), The

Nun's Priest describes the fox as a murderer and compares him to the greatest traitors in history (460–3). What is being mocked by these disproportionate comparisons? Is it Chauntecleer, who is far less important than he thinks? Is it the art of rhetoric with its emphasis on the amplification of subject-matter (in that amplification is inappropriate here)?

449   **col-fox**   fox with black markings (on the feet and the tips of the ears and tail).

   sly iniquitee   deceitful wickedness. Already overstated?

450   **woned**   lived, remained.

451   The elements of this phrase are a little hard to reconcile. *Ymaginacioun* is the part of the human mind which creates images of things either not actually present or not yet in existence. *Forncast* usually means 'planned beforehand'. So the phrase could mean 'planned beforehand by divine foresight' (if you regard *forncast* as the most important word) or 'foreseen by the noble imagination' (putting the emphasis on *ymaginacioun* and referring to Chauntecleer's dream). Perhaps the former is more mock-heroic.

452   **hegges**   hedges. The *same nyght* as Chauntecleer's dream.

454   **wont... to repaire**   accustomed to go.

455   **wortes**   cabbages (mentioned in the *Roman de Renart*).

456   **undren**   undern (originally meant 9 a.m., later meant mid-morning).

458   **gladly**   usually, willingly.

459   **liggen**   lie.

   mordre   murder.

460   The apostrophe indicates The Nun's Priest's passionate exclamation against the fox's treachery. The style is out of proportion with the thing described, just as the comparisons are. (See Interpretations, p. 110.)

461   **Scariot**   Judas Iscariot, who betrayed Jesus in the Bible.

   Genylon   Ganelon, who betrayed Charlemagne in the eleventh-century French epic, the *Chanson de Roland* (Song of Roland).

462   **dissymulour**   deceiver.

   Synon   Sinon, who tricked the Trojans into taking the wooden

horse into Troy, thus causing the fall of the city in Virgil's
Aeneid, book 2. Notice that The Nun's Priest chooses biblical,
medieval, and classical examples. (Compare with lines 344–90.)
463 **outrely**   utterly, completely.

The Nun's Priest on dreams and predestination: lines 464–84

The Nun's Priest blames Chauntecleer for failing to pay attention
to the warning in his dream. This leads him on to the larger
question of whether God's foreknowledge of all events means
that human beings (and presumably also chickens) have no free
will. The argument would be that if God has foreknowledge,
then He could see from the beginning of the universe everything
that would ever happen. If this is the case, none of our intentions
or actions can make any difference to what God saw from the
beginning, and there is no free will. Against this it could be
argued that God in relation to time is like a person on a hill in
relation to place. He sees what happens (or will happen) but He
does not control or influence it. (See Interpretations, p. 109.)

The Nun's Priest's elaborate statement that he does not
intend to go into the complexities of this issue in fact serves as a
sketch of the debate, but this is more like playful allusion than
serious argument. It is true that the question of the freedom of
the will was a much debated issue in fourteenth-century
universities (471), and that St Augustine, Boethius, and Thomas
Bradwardine were three of the principal authorities (475–6). The
Nun's Priest even outlines three of the main positions accurately
(477–84), but only to say that he will not discuss the issue (474,
485). In part, this is the rhetorical figure of *occupatio*, saying you
will not say something while actually giving an outline. But it is
also another variation on the mock-heroic, playing with the
contrast between the farmyard scene and the intellectual debate
it apparently exemplifies.

468 **forwoot** foreknows.

moot nedes must necessarily. It is worth asking how this transition works. The Nun's Priest criticizes Chauntecleer for ignoring the reliable warning in his dream. Then he says that what God sees will happen. This seems to equate the dream with what God sees, and indeed some dreams were thought of as messages from God. In that case the reliability of God's knowledge is contrasted with the folly of not heeding the warning. But the idea of necessity could also be applied to Chauntecleer's response. He was warned by his dream, but the warning was bound to be futile because God had already seen that the fox would carry him off. Clearly there are links between questions about dreams and questions about predestination, but Chaucer does not spell out exactly how he moves from one favourite topic to the other.

469 **after** according to.

clerkis learned men, scholars.

470–2 Any competent scholar will tell you that there is great disagreement and debate in the university on this subject.

474 To boult (*bulte*) flour is to sift it from the bran, so this line translates as, 'But I am not able to get to the heart of the matter'.

475 St Augustine of Hippo (354–430 AD), one of the four doctors (or teachers) of the Church, discussed the issue of free will in his attacks on Pelagius (active 399–418 AD). Pelagius believed that each person was free to choose between good and evil, and that if a Christian freely chose good, he or she would go to heaven. Arguing against Pelagius and his followers, Augustine insisted that people were corrupted from birth because of original sin and that they needed the freely given grace of God in order to be saved from hell. In his most famous work, *The City of God*, however, Augustine maintains that the freedom of the individual will is quite consistent with God's foreknowledge.

476 Boethius (*Boece*) lived from about 480 to 524 AD. His most famous work, *On the Consolation of Philosophy*, which Chaucer translated, upholds the freedom of the will. Thomas Bradwardine, who died in 1349, shortly after being appointed Archbishop of Canterbury, in his *On the Nature of God*,

Against the Pelagians, argued that human sinfulness required
the grace of God in order to be forgiven. His views left little
freedom for the human will.

477–84 The Nun's Priest sets out three possible views. Either God's
foreknowledge constrains (*streyneth* [478]) human actions
through simple necessity (477–9), or the human will is free in
spite of God's foreknowledge (480–1), or God's
foreknowledge constrains human freedom only with
conditional necessity (483–4). The distinction between simple
and conditional necessity comes from Boethius' *On the
Consolation of Philosophy* (Book 5, Prose Section 6). Dame
Philosophy distinguishes between things which are inevitable
(a person will die) and things that depend on choice (a person
will go for a walk). Now if you see someone walking, they
must be walking, but the fact that you see them walking was
not the thing that made them walk. Applying the same
argument to God, who can see through time as we see
through space, if He sees that a person will go for a walk, that
person must go for a walk, but God's knowledge that the
person will go for a walk is not the cause. This means there is
necessity (he must go for a walk), but only conditional
necessity (God's knowledge was not the cause). You can read
Chaucer's translation of this passage in *The Riverside Chaucer*,
p. 468, lines 177–213. Not everybody found this distinction
convincing, but it enabled some philosophers to preserve a
small space for human freedom while acknowledging God's
absolute knowledge and power.

477 **worthy forwityng**   noble foreknowledge.

478 **nedely**   necessarily.

479 **clepe**   call.

482 **wroght**   created.

483 **wityng**   knowledge.

   never a deel   not at all, not one bit.

484 Except by conditional necessity. What attitude do the next
two lines take to the philosophical issues The Nun's Priest has
just raised?

The Nun's Priest on women's advice: lines 485–500

Having brought up the issue of predestination, The Nun's Priest wants to leave it on one side and return to his narrative. After all he is only talking about a cockerel. But even the summary of the story so far, which he offers as preliminary to moving on, raises another general issue worthy of comment: women's advice (490–3). As soon as he has made his chauvinist observations on the bad consequences of women's advice, he remembers the women in the audience and distances himself from his own words. He was only joking (496). You can see what writers have to say on this topic (497–8). They are the cockerel's words and not his (499). Do these remarks succeed in avoiding blame, or does the offence remain? What does The Nun's Priest really think of women? (See Interpretations, pp. 119–20.)

485 **swich mateere**   this type of subject.
487 **with sorwe**   with sad results, to his sorrow.
489 **met**   dreamed.
490 **colde**   disastrous, fatal. Apparently this was a Viking proverb, but that did not prevent English writers from adopting it.
493 **Ther as**   where. The story of the fall is told in Genesis 3. Even in this story, which many women regard as offensively biased, it is not suggested that Adam was happy without Eve (see Genesis 2:20).
494–500 Is this really an apology or is the speaker making the offence worse? This semi-apology (or mock apology) is similar to a passage in the *Roman de la Rose* (lines 15195–214). In his edition Derek Pearsall points out that Chaucer himself often makes heavily ironic allusions to the debate about the position of women. He suggests that this comment may be typical of Chaucer, or even of medieval writing, rather than part of the character of The Nun's Priest.
494 **noot**   do not know. Of whom is he thinking?
496 **in my game**   as a joke.

497 Many authors (*auctours*) had written books criticizing women,
as *The Wife of Bath's Tale* and *The Merchant's Tale* show. You
can follow these ideas further in Alcuin Blamires's anthology,
Woman Defamed and Woman Defended.

499 The Nun's Priest now claims that he has merely been recording
Chauntecleer's thoughts. Narrators often summarize their
characters' thoughts without attribution, but The Nun's Priest's
claim looks like a smokescreen.

500 **divyne**   guess, suppose. Does this overstatement make the
whole passage ironic, or is he making fun of the apology he has
just made?

Chauntecleer notices the fox: lines 501–15

While Pertelote and his other wives roll in the sand and enjoy the
sun, Chauntecleer sings. Lazily he watches a butterfly fluttering
among the cabbages. Suddenly he is overcome by fear as he
sees the fox. He crows twice and jumps up. The Nun's Priest
continues to interrupt his story with learned allusions, this time
to natural history (the singing of mermaids and the instinctive
fear of the predator). Or are these interruptions? Perhaps The
Nun's Priest tells his story in order to display the breadth of his
knowledge. But the story itself tends to deflate learning,
including the learning which The Nun's Priest likes to show off.

501 **soond**   sand. Hens often roll around on the ground (perhaps
trying to rub off parasites). This is called a 'dustbath'.
bathe hire   immerse herself, rub herself.

502 **Lith**   lies.

503 **Agayn**   in, facing.
free   noble, generous. (Compare with line 148.)

504 **murier**   more tunefully. Medieval bestiaries (handbooks
describing animals, real and imaginary, usually with moral
commentary) explain that mermaids, like the sirens of Greek
mythology, sing to sailors and attempt to lure them to

destruction on the rocks on which the mermaids lie. The comparison with mermaids may convey an idea of the danger (to himself) of Chauntecleer's singing.

505 *Phisiologus* is the title (sometimes treated as the author) of a handbook of animals which was probably composed in Greek in the second century AD, but which was known throughout the Middle Ages in a Latin version. Chaucer need not have known this work; he could have taken all that appears here from a medieval encyclopaedia, for example the *Speculum doctrinale* (Mirror of Learning) of Vincent of Beauvais (about 1190 to approximately 1264).

508 **boterflye** butterfly.

510 He had no desire at all to crow then.

511 *Cok! cok!* is an imitation of the cockerel's cry of alarm.

512 **affrayed** afraid.

514 The fox is the cockerel's contrary (*contrarie*) because he is the predator who seeks to destroy him.

515 **erst** before. Chauntecleer instinctively fears the fox. (Compare with lines 129–140.)

The fox's flattering speech: lines 516–64

Chauntecleer means to fly away as soon as he sees the fox, but he is deflected from his purpose by the fox's words. The fox begins by assuring Chauntecleer of his good intentions. He has come only to listen to the cock's singing. Then he tries to reassure him by claiming that he is a friend of the family. He reinforces this by praising the singing of Chauntecleer's father and describing his technique in some detail, laying particular stress on the closed eyes. Finally, he invites Chauntecleer to demonstrate his prowess in singing by imitating his father. Chauntecleer is flattered by the fox's words and decides to do as he suggests. The narrator warns the audience of the dangers of flattery. The arguments Chaucer's fox uses are closely based on those in the *Roman de Renart*, though Renart goes as far as to claim that he and Chauntecleer are related.

520 **feend**   devil.

521 If I intended any harm or discourtesy towards you.

522 **conseil**   secrets.

   t'espye   to spy out.

527 **Therwith**   in addition.

528 **Boethius** (*Boece*) also composed a treatise *On Music*, which was
   used as part of the course in music at medieval universities.
   The theory of music was one of the four subjects of the
   quadrivium, the mathematical part of the arts course. (The
   other mathematical subjects were geometry, arithmetic and
   astronomy.) Here the fox is just name-dropping, citing the best-
   known medieval authority on the theory of music. The idea of
   a fox talking about the singing voice of a famous, long-dead
   music theorist would probably have amused the more learned
   listeners. (Compare with line 476.)

530 **hire**   their.

531 **ese**   pleasure. There is only one way that either of
   Chauntecleer's parents would have been to the fox's house, and
   it has nothing to do with *gentillesse*.

532 **fayn**   gladly.

533 But since we are talking about singing. *Men speke* has an
   impersonal force here: 'one spoke', 'something has been said'.

534 As I may use my two eyes well. Why is this oath by the fox's
   eyes?

535 **Save**   apart from.

537 **of herte**   from the heart, full of emotion.

539 **so peyne hym**   take such pains, make such an effort.

540 **wynke**   close the eyes (that is, keep them closed, unlike the
   Modern English 'wink').

541 **tiptoon**   tiptoes.

543 **discrecioun**   understanding, sound judgement.

545 **passe**   surpass.

546 The reference is to a late twelfth-century Latin satirical poem,
   Burnellus or the Mirror of Fools, by Nigel Wireker. The chief
   character of the poem is an ass named Burnellus (in English,
   little brown), who is trying to obtain a longer tail. The incident
   which Chaucer describes forms a subplot, showing the
   ingenuity of a cock in taking revenge on a man who injured
   him five years previously. To get his own back, the cock

decided not to crow on time. This caused his victim to oversleep and miss the service at which he would have been made a bishop.

549 **nyce** foolish (the priest's son, that is).

550 **benefice** church job.

553 **his subtiltee** the ingenuity of the cock in the story.

554 **for seinte charitee** for holy charity, for the love of God.

555 **Lat se** show me.

countrefete imitate (without the implication of deceit which this word has in Modern English).

557 **As man** like one. (Compare with lines 121, 533.)

558 **ravysshed with** overcome, seduced by.

559–64 Some critics take the address to lords (none of whom are present) as evidence that this aside is addressed by Chaucer to his audience rather than by The Nun's Priest to his. Others point out that it might be The Nun's Priest using 'lords' as a rhetorical exaggeration.

559 **flatour** flatterer.

560 **losengeour** flatterer, deceiver.

564 There is no passage in Ecclesiastes (one of the books of the Bible) which relates to flatterers, but there is an appropriate passage in Proverbs 29:5, another book of the Bible, also written by Solomon.

The fox seizes Chauntecleer: lines 565–608

Tricked by the fox's flattery, Chauntecleer shuts his eyes to sing his best. The fox seizes him and carries him off to the woods, much to the distress of Pertelote and the other hens. The Nun's Priest amplifies this tragic turn of events with three apostrophes (to destiny, to Venus, and to Geoffrey de Vinsauf, his rhetorical model), and three historical comparisons (the fall of Troy, the fall of Carthage, and Nero's destruction of Rome). What is the effect of comparing such grand events with the story of a chicken? (See Interpretations, p. 110.)

567 **for the nones**   for the purpose.

568 Finally, the fox is named as Master Russell. Russell means 'little red'. (Compare this with Burnellus in Note to line 546, p. 73.) Some critics regard this name as evidence that Chaucer did not have direct access to the *Roman de Renart*; others think he was deliberately avoiding the name of his source's hero.

569 **gargat**   throat.

570 **beer**   carried.

571 **sewed**   followed, pursued.

572–5 The first mock-heroic apostrophe ('O destiny') pretends to see Chauntecleer's whole fate mapped out in advance. If only he had remained on his beam, petrified with fear. If only his wife had believed in dreams. Naturally, this misfortune would occur on a Friday, traditionally seen as an unlucky day. Is Chaucer being ironic at the expense of people who interpret like this, or should we see the expression as purely comic?

576–80 The Nun's Priest turns to Venus (addressed as the goddess of pleasure, rather than of love) to accuse her of betraying her faithful servant and allowing him to be tormented on her day.

577–8 Chauntecleer serves Venus because he is so assiduous to his seven wives, but the word also relates to courtly love, in which the lover is the 'servant' of the lady. 'Service' as a euphemism for sexual intercourse gives the ambiguity of these expressions a less courtly turn.

579 According to medieval Christian thinking sexual activity could only avoid being sinful if it was engaged in without emotion and for the purpose of having children (*to multiplye*), but Chauntecleer, as a good cockerel, has sex mainly for pleasure (*delit*). Again the joke depends on suggesting (but then refusing) human norms which are quite inapplicable in the farmyard.

580 **woldestow**   would you. Friday is Venus' day. Compare with *vendredi* (French), *venerdi* (Italian). English Friday is so called from Freya, the Viking goddess corresponding to Venus.

581–8 The Nun's Priest calls on Geoffrey de Vinsauf, author of the treatise on writing poetry *Poetria nova* (New Poetics), both because as a skilled rhetorician he would be better able to amplify the tragedy of the cock's presumed death, and

because one of the examples in *New Poetics* is a lament for
the death of Richard I, who was mortally wounded by an
arrow on Friday 26 March 1199. At more than 60 lines
Geoffrey's Latin lament is too long to quote here, but it too
makes heavy use of apostrophe, for example:

> **O tearful day of Venus! O bitter star!**
> **That day was your night, and that Venus your poison,**
> **That day gave you the wound.**   **(lines 375–7)**

For an international tragedy, which Richard's death was, such
a highly-wrought formal lament was appropriate (even if its
form seems artificial by our standards); in the farmyard it is
ludicrous, which is the joke throughout the tale.

581 **maister soverayn** supreme master.

583 **compleynedest** lamented.

584 **sentence** intelligence, judgement.

587 **Thanne** then (if I had Geoffrey's skill).
    pleyne lament.

589 The Nun's Priest moves from apostrophe to comparison. The
    lamentation of the hens was greater than that of the Trojan
    women at the fall of Ilium (*Ylion* [590]) or Troy. The Nun's
    Priest makes particular reference to the retelling of this story
    by Virgil (*Aeneid*, Book 2, lines 453–558; the lamentation of
    the women is at 486–90). (Compare with Note to line 462,
    p. 66.) (See Interpretations, p. 98–9.)

591 **Pirrus** Pyrrhus, was the son of Achilles, the greatest hero
    on the Greek side, who was dead by the time Troy was
    captured. Pyrrhus killed the aged Trojan king Priam in front
    of the altars of his family, at the centre of the citadel.
    streite drawn.

593 *Eneydos* the *Aeneid*. Although Virgil's Latin epic poem is
    mainly concerned with the founding of Rome, it includes an
    account of the fall of Troy, told by Aeneas, who fled from
    the ruins of the city. What is the effect of comparing the
    clucking of the hens to one of the most famous passages of
    Latin poetry?

596 **shrighte** shrieked.

597 Hasdrubal was the Carthaginian leader defeated by the

Roman general Scipio Africanus Minor in 146 BC (see Note
to line 357, p. 59). Rome and Carthage had been at war since
264 BC (the so-called Punic Wars), but Rome only destroyed
Cathage in 146. According to Valerius Maximus (see Notes,
p. 54), the defenders of Carthage had decided to kill
themselves, but Hasdrubal surrendered to Scipio. His wife
was angry at his weakness and threw herself and their sons
into the flames. But Chaucer seems to be using a different
version of the story, probably the one in St Jerome's *Letter
Against Jovinianus* (written about 393 AD, and a book
Chaucer often used), which describes the virtue and loyalty
of Hasdrubal's wife in preferring death to dishonour (and
omits her criticism of his cowardice).

599 **brend** burned.

604 Most historians blame the great fire at Rome in 64 AD on the
emperor Nero, though he used the fire as an excuse for
persecuting the Christians. Boethius' *On the Consolation of
Philosophy* (see Note to line 476, p. 68), which Chaucer
certainly knew, mentions Nero's role in burning the city and
murdering the senators (Book 2, Poem 6).

607 It is the senators who are innocent (*Withouten gilt*), not Nero.

608 Is this comment helpful to the audience, or has The Nun's
Priest finally become self-conscious about all the
interruptions to the tale?

Everyone chases the fox: lines 609–35

The widow and her daughters hear the shrieking of the hens and
see the fox carrying the cock away. They shout and chase after
him with their neighbours and their dogs. The noise disturbs the
other animals, who add to a rising cacophony fit for the end of
the world. The story demands a chase and the sources provide
one, but Chaucer adds many details, especially lists of names
and animals (and even a comparison). The whole movement of
the verse seems to change, more patterned and faster, more
breathless, crammed full of names, verbs and noises.

609 **sely** poor, simple.

614 **weylaway** woe, alas.

616 **staves** sticks.

617 Talbot and Gerland are also dogs. What is the effect of giving their names?

618 The distaff (the stick on which the wool is wound in hand-spinning) would usually be held by the housewife, so perhaps *Malkyn* (diminutive of Matilda) is the widow's name.

619–22 The domestic animals add to the chaos of the chase scene, but they run away because they are frightened by the noise of the dogs and the people; they do not chase after the fox.

619 **eek the verray hogges** even the pigs.

620 **So fered for** so frightened because of.

622 They ran so hard it seemed to them that their hearts would burst.

623 **yolleden** screeched.
feendes devils. Grammatically this should be the animals, but perhaps we should also associate it with the people in view of lines 628, 636, and contemporary reports of the noise made in the Peasants' Revolt. (See Note to line 628 below.)

624 **as... quelle** as if they were going to be killed.

625 **flowen** flew.

627 **a, benedicitee** O, bless us (Latin).

628 **meynee** crowd, rabble. Jack Straw was one of the leaders of the Peasants' Revolt (1381), who was later hanged for his part in the rebellion. The revolt was sparked by discontent at taxation (particularly at the poll tax of 1379 and 1380), but became an attack on law, learning and foreigners, as well as an opportunity to settle old scores. The peasants broke into John of Gaunt's palace of the Savoy, destroyed government records at the New Temple, broke open the prisons and beheaded the Lord Treasurer and the Archbishop of Canterbury, as well as minor officials and tax-collectors. Chaucer was present in London, in his apartment above Aldgate, throughout the rebellion. As a customs official and a man of learning he must have been a potential victim of the violence. This is the only definite reference Chaucer makes to those events.

630 Flemish people (from Flanders, roughly modern Belgium) had been encouraged to settle in London earlier in the fourteenth

century. They were mainly involved in the wool trade and
some of them were very prosperous. As a wealthy minority
they became a target for the rebels' wrath. It appears that
around 40 Flemish people were dragged from sanctuary in the
Church of St Martin's in the Vintry and beheaded. Their
headless bodies were piled in Thames Street, near Chaucer's
family house. Perhaps the reference to the Flemish expresses
Chaucer's abhorrence at the way the violence of the Revolt
affected him. Or it may avoid discussion of the political
grievances, which caused the peasants to rebel, by accusing
them of random violence. What is the effect of the return to
the mock-heroic in the next line?

632 **bemes** trumpets.
    box boxwood.
633 **powped** puffed. Perhaps all these instruments make the
    chase after the fox seem like a village festival or like an army
    marching.
634 **skriked** shrieked.
    howped whooped.
635 Should we take this as a hyperbole about the sound (like the
    last trumpet) or is this another reference to the noise and
    violence of 1381?

Chauntecleer's escape and the moral of the tale: lines 636–80

Chauntecleer urges the fox to make a speech of defiance to his
pursuers, even suggesting a few phrases which might appeal to
him. As the fox opens his mouth to agree, Chauntecleer escapes
and flies away. At once the fox apologizes for his actions and asks
the cock to return so that he can explain. Chauntecleer replies
that he has learned his lesson and will not again be deceived
through flattery. This prompts the fox to outline the lesson he has
learned: that one should know when to be silent. The narrator
then explains that his story is an example of the consequences of
carelessness and trusting in flattery. All these moral comments fit

in easily with the mock-heroic approach of the tale. They are all sufficiently obvious and overstated to be funny. But in the last nine lines The Nun's Priest (or is it Chaucer?) appears to turn on his audience. All those of you who think this is a funny story about a hen and a fox should take note of its moral teaching. For as St Paul says, everything that is written is written in order to teach us. The tale then concludes with a prayer.

There seem to be two ways to take this. Either the tactics of the whole poem are turned on their head at the end and we are invited to take seriously the moral comment we have been laughing at throughout, or the concluding passage is the climax of the comic interruptions, when the whole idea of moralizing every story is ridiculed. Which of these alternatives do you prefer, or can you see a way of combining them? The argument against the first alternative is that, even on a rereading, the moral comments offered in the tale are mostly banal or inappropriate. The argument against the second view is that it is hard to see either Chaucer or The Nun's Priest openly mocking the words of St Paul or undercutting the final prayer in this way.

Possibly, one could construct a 'middle' reading of this passage by distinguishing between The Nun's Priest's voice and Chaucer's. Or perhaps the citation of St Paul serves to remind us that serious moral teaching can be drawn from simple stories, even though that has not been the intention of this story. This would have the effect of highlighting the question of the relationship between story and teaching which has been at issue from the beginning of this tale, and the relationship between meaning and enjoyment which is at issue throughout the storytelling competition. In several of his works Chaucer, who had trouble finishing poems, preferred suspended endings in which two apparently contrasting views are held simultaneously. In order to avoid being tied down to a simple moral statement (which is often implied in a straightforward ending), he openly stated (and often openly rejected) several alternatives. (See Interpretations, pp. 120–3.)

636 Should we draw any (moral or gender) implication from this repeated reference to 'good men'? (Compare with lines 674, 679.)

638 Anyone is Fortune's enemy at the point when she dashes their hopes.

641–7 Why does Chauntecleer elaborate so much on what the fox might like to say? Is he constructing a flattering self-image for the fox, or presenting himself (with comic unlikeliness) as the fox's friend?

641 **if that I were as ye** if I were in your position.

642 **as wys God helpe me** as surely as God may help me.

643 **Turneth agayn** turn back. Perhaps the reference to churls (peasants) takes us back to the comparison with the Peasants' Revolt (see Note to line 628, p. 78). *Daun Russell* [568] is invited to see himself as the noble disdaining the mob.

644 **pestilence** plague.

645 **wodes syde** edge of the wood.

646 **Maugree youre heed** in spite of anything you can do.

647 In acting his role for the fox, Chauntecleer insists that he will be eaten.

648 Contrast the fox's terse monosyllabic reply with the elaborate speech the cock offered him as enticement. But even one word wrecks the fox's plan.

650 **delyverly** quickly, nimbly.

654 **ydoon trespas** done an injury, wronged.

657 **wikke entente** evil intention. The fox still thinks he is resourceful enough (or Chauntecleer stupid enough) to make good his mistake.

660 **shrewe** beshrew, curse. Curse us both if I shall do that (that is, 'I shall never do it').

664 **Do me to synge** make me sing.

665–6 For may God never let someone thrive who deliberately shuts his eyes (*wynketh* [665]) when he should keep them open. The conclusion generalizes the idea so that *wynketh* conveys the idea of deliberate moral blindness. Do you think the references to God in these lines show us The Nun's Priest's voice emerging from the words of the animals?

668 **undiscreet** careless, foolish.
governaunce self-control.

669 **jangleth**   talks, chatters. Notice how the fox generalizes the
    moral.

670 **recchelees**   thoughtless, careless. With this word and negligent
    (*necligent* [671]) the narrator extends his comment to cover all
    the acts of folly in the tale, including the disregarded dreams.

672 But you who consider this tale a foolish trifle. In his edition
    Derek Pearsall suggests that this line (and therefore what
    follows) may be addressed only to those who dismiss the tale,
    in which case only the straitlaced would be subject to the
    dilemma of the final lines. But they could be addressed to
    anyone who finds the tale amusing.

674 **Taketh the moralite**   understand the moral lesson.

675 The reference is to St Paul's Epistle to the Romans 15:4: *For
    whatever was written was written for our instruction.* St Paul
    (martyred near Rome around 65 AD) was a persecutor of
    Christians who was converted to Christianity and became the
    most important early Christian missionary. The letters (epistles)
    which he wrote to individuals and to particular churches have
    been accepted as part of the Christian Bible with the full
    authority which follows from that. Some modern writers
    believe that his prejudices (particularly against women) have
    unduly influenced Christian teaching.

677 This line combines two conventional Christian images
    describing the technique of interpretation. One image concerns
    the grain (or sometimes the kernel of a nut), which must be
    found and cherished, as opposed to the chaff or husk
    (sometimes the shell of the nut), which must be thrown away.
    In these images we are instructed to read through the surface of
    a text so as to capture its inner meaning, discarding elements
    of the surface which do not form part of the inner truth. St
    Augustine (see Note to line 475, p. 68) in his *On Christian
    Doctrine* (3.5.9) explains the idea in more detail. In the other
    image, fruit is the worthy product of something good, as in
    Christ's parable of the fruit trees (Matthew 7:15–20). But the
    main point in this context is that interpretation can take
    something morally valuable (fruit or grain) even from
    something apparently worthless (the chaff).

Of course the chaff is also an important aspect of storytelling. In his attack on *The Monk's Tale*, in *The Nun's Priest's*

Prologue (35–6), The Host pointed out that if you lose the
attention of your audience the moral goes for nothing.

679 Probably we should take the phrase *As seith my lord* as a device
to fill out the line. It might refer either to The Nun's Priest's
superior within the church or, perhaps less likely, to The
Prioress, his employer.

680 Do you regard this ending as conventional or as genuinely
pious?

Epilogue to The Nun's Priest's Tale

The Host congratulates The Nun's Priest on his tale: lines 681–96

The Host suggests that if the teller of the tale were not a priest he would have as many 'hens' as Chauntecleer. He starts to compare The Nun's Priest's long neck, large chest, sharp eyes, and red colouring with Chauntecleer. What do you think of the idea of a similarity between The Nun's Priest and Chauntecleer? What does The Host's obscene wordplay (682, 685) tell us about his response to the tale or to The Nun's Priest? Finally, The Host turns to the next storyteller. In most manuscripts the next tale is *The Second Nun's Tale*, which tells the life of St Cecilia. Some critics think that Chaucer originally intended to go on to *The Wife of Bath's Prologue*, with its frank discussion of marriage and The Wife's treatment of her five husbands. Perhaps this would explain The Host's crude language here.

The Epilogue is not in the Hengwrt or Ellesmere manuscripts (see Notes, p. 31) and appears in only one group of manuscripts. Most scholars think that Chaucer wrote these lines (with the exception of lines 695–6, probably composed by a scribe) but later cancelled them because in them The Host makes the same jokes about priests and sex as he does in *The Monk's Prologue* (1924–64). (See Interpretations, p. 123.)

681 **breche** buttocks.
     stoon testicle.
684 **seculer** secular (not a priest and therefore not committed to celibacy).
685 **trede-foul** lover of hens, lecher. Do you think there is any evidence in The Nun's Priest's behaviour to suggest this? Perhaps The Host is joking about it because it is so unlikely, or perhaps he thinks that The Nun's Priest has said too much

about marriage for someone with no experience of it.
aright truly.
686 **corage** heart, sexual desire.
Myght strength.
687 **Thee were nede** you would need. The Host may be suggesting that the sisters of the convent are The Nun's Priest's hens.
688 **Ya** yes. (Compare with lines 100 and 107.)
689 **braunes** muscles.
691 **sperhauk** sparrowhawk.
yen eyes.
693 **brasile** brazil wood (bright-red dye). Presumably The Nun's Priest, who is not described elsewhere, shares Chauntecleer's red complexion. There was also a strong emphasis on redness in Chauntecleer's dream and Pertelote's interpretation of it (136, 160–6).
694 **faire falle yow** good luck to you.
696 **shuln** shall. This word is uncharacteristic of Chaucer.

Interpretations

Setting and genre

Setting the tale in context

In the *General Prologue* Chaucer describes the fictional pilgrims who become the storytellers of *The Canterbury Tales*. Many of the pilgrims' portraits are very detailed, telling us of their background, rank in society, occupation and appearance. As the creator of these characters, Chaucer shows his very shrewd understanding of fourteenth-century society. He also reveals a keen sense of ironic humour, sometimes delighting in the differences between how people might be expected to behave and how they actually do. You can read more about the pilgrimage in the Notes, p. 29.

Some of the pilgrims tell stories in keeping with their character. The *verray, parfit gentil knyght* (*General Prologue*, 72) for example, who loves *chivalrie,/Trouthe and honour, fredom and curteisie* (*General Prologue*, 45–6), tells a noble tale of battle and romance, but others, like The Monk, who loves hunting, fine clothes and good food, tell tedious stories which do not live up to expectations.

Rather unusually, the description of The Nun's Priest in the *General Prologue* is not much help as a starting point for understanding his tale. Chaucer tells us nothing about The Nun's Priest apart from the very brief comment that The Prioress was well-attended:

> Another NONNE with hire hadde she,
> That was hir chapeleyne, and preestes thre.   (163–4)

The Nun's Priest, who tells the tale of Chauntecleer and Pertelote, is one of these three priests and that is almost all we know about him before he begins his tale. Though it might be amusing to note a similarity between Chauntecleer in a farmyard of hens and The Nun's Priest in a convent of nuns, the observation does not help us much in understanding the purpose of the tale. Perhaps Chaucer deliberately tells us nothing about The Nun's Priest so that the tale's unexpectedness may have greater impact.

Stories can stand on their own, of course, but more often in story collections their meaning comes from either their relationship with their teller or with the tales which precede or follow them. You may find a clue as to why Chaucer has The Nun's Priest tell the story of Chauntecleer and Pertelote at this particular point if you look at *The Monk's Tale*, which precedes it.

The Monk had informed – or forewarned – the pilgrims of the content and purpose of his tale at the outset:

> I wol biwaille in manere of tragedie
> The harm of hem that stoode in heigh degree,
> And fillen so that ther nas no remedie
> To brynge hem out of hit adversitee.
>
> (*The Monk's Tale*, [1991–1994])

True to intent, he demonstrates the harsh dealings of the goddess Fortune with such as Lucifer, Adam, Samson, Hercules and Croesus as a result of their pride. For example:

> Anhanged was Cresus, the proude kyng;
> His roial trone myghte hym nat availle.
> Tragedies noon oother maner thyng...
> ...Fortune alwey wole assaille
> With unwar strook the regnes that been proude...
>
> (*The Monk's Tale*, [2759–2764])

This typifies the tone of the 17 tragedies, which The Monk recounts from the *hundred in my celle* (*The Prologue of The Monk's Tale*, [1972]) before The Knight brings The Monk abruptly to a halt with: '*Hoo... good sire, namoore of this!*' (*The Nun's Priest's Prologue*, [1]).

The link between *The Monk's Tale* and *The Nun's Priest's Tale*

The links between the tales are part of the dramatic framework of *The Canterbury Tales*. They are a useful literary device that allows the pilgrims – and Chaucer – to respond to the stories they have heard, to anticipate the next story and for us to test our reactions and expectations against theirs. Between *The Monk's Tale* and *The Nun's Priest's Tale* there is a lively exchange between The Knight, The Host, The Monk and The Nun's Priest. (See *The Nun's Priest's Prologue*.)

The Knight and The Host object strongly to *The Monk's Tale*. They are clearly very irritated by the futile and tedious monotony of The Monk's catalogue of woe.

Activity

Look closely at *The Nun's Priest's Prologue* and consider these questions:
- What are The Knight's objections to *The Monk's Tale*? (1–13)
- What are The Host's criticisms? (14–38)
- What kind of story is expected from The Nun's Priest? (44–9)

Discussion

Both The Knight and The Host react quite forcefully to The Monk and his tale, though The Knight's observations are more general than The Host's personal and specific attack. Their very critical comments tell us as much about the kind of story each wants to hear next as they do about their response to the story they have just heard.

The Knight's objections go beyond audience fatigue. He argues that folk want to hear stories with happy endings, in which *prosperitee* (11) follows *adversitee* (*The Monk's Tale*, [1994]), and asks for a *gladsom* (12) tale, where fortune's wheel lifts up as well as overthrows. He suggests that it would be *goodly for to telle* (13) a story of good fortune which gives joy and delight. Do you think that The Knight is seriously asking for a story that balances The Monk's tragic view of life or is Chaucer preparing the way for a story which he knows will meet The Knight's demands though perhaps not quite in the way he expects?

The Host disapproves of the tedious pessimism of The Monk's tragedies. Notice the change in tone when he interrupts The Knight. On a personal level he is quite rude about both the content and the style of The Monk's story:

> '.. this Monk he clappeth lowde
> ...it is a peyne,
> As ye han seyd, to heere of hevynesse.'   (15–21)

In the *General Prologue*, The Monk is presented not as a devout and learned scholar but as a man who loved hunting and good living. Perhaps The Host feels let down by *The Monk's Tale* and the lack of entertainment when there is *no desport ne game* (25). After all, the story-telling competition had been The Host's idea and he is responsible for its success. The prize was to be given to the pilgrim who told the most instructive and enjoyable tale, *of best sentence and moost solaas* (*General Prologue*, [798]). The Host bluntly dismisses the tone, style, content, social and moral function of *The Monk's Tale* as *nat worth a boterflye* (24).

When The Host challenges The Nun's Priest, even though his horse may give the appearance to the contrary, to *Be blithe* (46) and make *hertes glade* (45) The Nun's Priest knows that unless *I be myrie, ywis I wol be blamed* (51).

Genre

You will find an introduction to the genres of *The Nun's Priest's Tale* in the Notes, p. 37. Genre means 'kind of writing' and the term is used to define how a writer gives his or her writing its form and shape. Traditionally, there have been certain fixed genres – for example, tragedy, romance, epic – each with distinctive conventions and characteristic styles of writing, though in the last two centuries we have seen literary works which do not belong to any one genre. Instead there has been a growing belief that content and purpose determine the form and style of a literary work.

In *The Canterbury Tales* as a whole we have a range of very different kinds of tales – romance, *fabliau*, parable, fable. By the time Chaucer came to write *The Nun's Priest's Tale*, he had shown that he could be courtly and serious on the one hand, and realistic and humorous on the other. It is difficult to fit *The Nun's Priest's Tale* comfortably into any one genre because within the tale itself Chaucer adopts and adapts a number of different genres and moves from one style to another, sometimes simultaneously. The effect is similar to a kaleidoscope where the depth of colour and meaning comes from the way in which two or more elements are put together.

The beast-fable

In *The Nun's Priest's Tale*, Chaucer uses many of the features of the beast-fable genre. (See Notes, pp. 44–45.) A fable is a short story using animals as characters to illustrate a moral principle that is usually made explicit at the end by the narrator or one of the characters. In most fables the protagonists are talking birds or animals whose words and actions reflect human behaviour, exemplifying virtues such as patience or prudence and vices such as pride, envy or greed. By the fourteenth century, the fable had become a familiar form of storytelling and a popular source of entertainment. It had also become a well-established literary type, used in the schoolroom to teach composition and literary devices, including structure and rhetoric. Some medieval preachers used fables as examples to illustrate a moral truth in a visual and often humorous way.

In its simplest form, the beast-fable conveys a practical, moral message. In the example in the Appendix (p. 159), a fox flatters a crow into singing so that the crow drops the meat it is eating, the moral being to remain alert, to avoid vanity and to keep your mouth shut. The trick is being able to see how one thing represents another.

As the medieval fable developed, it became more sophisticated. In France, in the twelfth century, a whole cycle of animal stories grew around the central character of Renard the Fox and an oral storytelling tradition in the vernacular attracted a wider audience than scholars and the nobility. Animals became characters with personalities and human emotions; motives and actions became plots. Such developments can be comic because the incongruity between what things are and what they ought to be can be explored more fully. The fable is a flexible genre which can serve a range of purposes. For example, it can be used to make a political point, as in *Animal Farm*, where George Orwell satirizes human behaviour by making the differences between the animals and humans scarcely recognizable.

You will find an extract from the French *Roman de Renart* collection of stories, commonly thought to be Chaucer's main source for this tale, in the Appendix, p. 159, but there are many other examples of fables which you may like to research for yourself.

Comparing *The Nun's Priest's Tale* with the summary of the episode from the *Roman de Renart* in the Appendix will help you to begin to work out how Chaucer develops the beast-fable for his own purposes. (See also the Notes, p. 63.)

Activity

- Read the extract from the *Roman de Renart* in the Appendix, pages 164–5.
- Using the headings of (a) plot and (b) character, note the main points of difference between the *Roman de Renart* version of the cock and the fox story and *The Nun's Priest's Tale*.

Discussion

Chaucer takes the skeletal plot – a cockerel has a dream that he saw *a beest/Was lyk an hound* (133–4) – he ignores his own interpretation and so fails to recognize the fox as the enemy of his dream. The fox flatters him into closing his eyes and in turn the cock flatters the fox into opening his mouth. The cock escapes and the fox loses a meal. But Chaucer so substantially elaborates the story that in *The Nun's Priest's Tale* the fox doesn't make his appearance in the farmyard until almost the end of the story and the actual plot accounts for less than a tenth of the tale as a whole.

Signout oi auez mãir que
pu mãir conour w moir
meur puis mur belanie

The fox seizes a large white cockerel by the throat. This illustration and
the next are taken from manuscripts of the *Roman de Renart*, Chaucer's
principal source for the tale.

The widow chases the fox, and the cockerel escapes.

In the *Roman de Renart*, the animal and human worlds remain separate though the moral is applicable to human behaviour. In *The Nun's Priest's Tale*, however, the birds and animals are psychologically plausible human beings at the same time as displaying behaviour consistent with the animal world they represent. Chauntecleer and Pertelote have human emotions and animal instincts simultaneously.

Activity

This activity asks you to look at a short passage from *The Nun's Priest's Tale* to consider how Chaucer develops Chauntecleer's character.
* Read lines 406–18.
* How does Chaucer present Chauntecleer in these lines?

Discussion

In many respects Chauntecleer's behaviour is what we might expect from a cockerel. He flies down from his perch (406), finds some corn (409) and *fethered Pertelote twenty tyme* (411). But his attitude is also psychologically very human. Essentially, Chauntecleer is trying to recover his macho image after dismissing Pertelote's advice to take some *laxatyf* (177). He copulates with Pertelote, proves his virility and thereby forgets the warning of his fearful dream.

> He looketh as it were a grym leoun,
> And on his toos he rometh up and doun;
> Hym deigned nat to sette his foot to grounde...
> And to hym rennen thanne his wyves alle.
> Thus roial, as a prince is in his halle... (413–18)

The Nun's Priest says, *My tale is of a cok* (486), from a time when *Beestes and briddes koude speke and synge* (115). Do you think we should take his claim to be telling a fable seriously or is it a thin disguise for presenting ideas which may ruffle more feathers than Chauntecleer's? Perhaps Chaucer, with tongue in cheek, is adapting the beast-fable genre for his own purposes which include laughing at human behaviour as well as at the genre itself.

As the critic Muscatine points out (Charles Muscatine, *Chaucer and the French Tradition*, p. 239), the difference between *The Nun's Priest's Tale* and animal fable:

is that this [tale] cannot long be taken more seriously in one
direction than in the other. Fable respects the boundary
between animal fiction and the human fiction it illustrates.
But the whole spirit of this poem is to erase or at least
overleap the boundaries: animal and human, fiction and truth
severally join and separate, change partners and flirt here.
The one constancy in the poem is this shifting of focus...

Activity

Look at what Chaucer has added to the beast-fable by tracking the
central plot through the story. It may help you to use the headings
below to sort out the plot from the added material. Some of the work
has been done for you to build on.

Lines	Plot	Description, digressions, examples, interludes
55–80		Description of the poor widow
81–115		Description of Chauntecleer and Pertelote
116–141	Chauntecleer's dream	
142–203		Pertelote's explanation of the dream's cause
204–217		Chauntecleer's belief in dreams
218–390		*Exempla* of prophetic dreams
391–420		
421–448		
449–459		
460–484		Digressions on treachery and predestination
485–500		
501–558		
559–564		
565–571		
572–608		
609–635	The chase	
636–671		
672–680		

Discussion

One of the things we notice is that the tale's structure is far more complex than the usual fable. The plot is not of central importance. As fast as we return to the plot we leave it again. Side by side with the story there is a wide range of digressions and allusions.

The Nun's Priest begins with a realistic description of the poor widow which is closely followed by a mock-heroic introduction to Chauntecleer and Pertelote. But contrary to expectation, Chauntecleer's terrifying dream leads us not into the action but Pertelote's treatise on medieval medicine and a scholarly debate on the significance of dreams, with *exempla* – examples – from classical stories, from the Bible and from legends of English saints (see Notes, p. 37 and pp. 53–6). Copulation and corn restore Chauntecleer's bravado and The Nun's Priest begins to *telle his aventure* (420). But the dating of the fateful day is embellished with further comment and allusion before the fox sneaks into the yard and hides among the cabbages (455). There follow yet further digressions on treachery, predestination and women before the fox flatters and seizes Chauntecleer. Much lamentation follows in mock-heroic vein before The Nun's Priest breathlessly tells how the widow, her daughters, farmhands and dogs give chase and how Chauntecleer escapes from the fox's jaws. The tale ends with The Nun's Priest offering a number of possible morals and coming to a swift end.

What is the effect of this? Do you think The Nun's Priest is deliberately tantalizing his audience with examples and digressions? (See Notes, p. 63.) Or is Chaucer intentionally exaggerating to make us laugh at the absurdity of such learning applied to a story of a cock and a fox? Is the effect to poke fun at the medieval art of composition or to parody the fable as a genre by treating what is really a secular subject with the earnestness of theological debate? Though The Nun's Priest's storytelling may appear out of control, Chaucer knows exactly what he is doing. Much of the added material does not advance the action but turns the poem into a mock-epic through the elevation of a barnyard incident into an event of universal significance.

This fifteenth-century misericord from Norwich Cathedral shows the widow and her dog chasing the fox, who has the cockerel in his mouth. Misericords are wood-carvings made on the underside of tipping seats in choir-stalls. They often illustrate secular stories. This beautiful English example shows that the story of the cock and the fox was very widely known.

The heroic and the mock-heroic

Another name for the epic is the heroic poem. Classical epics developed from ancient legend. The best-known examples are Homer's *Iliad* and *Odyssey*, and Virgil's *Aeneid*. One of the chief characteristics of the classical epic is that it tells the story of a hero, often a warrior, whose exploits help his country to victory. The epic hero's fate – and the fate of his nation – are the concern of the gods, who sometimes intervene to help him and sometimes watch him suffer. Extreme courage and valour or Fate determine the outcome according to the will of the gods. The epic hero is noble, brave, courageous and eloquent. His outstanding courage and reputation earn him the love of renowned ladies. The action of the epic or heroic poem is on a correspondingly grand scale and the style is elevated to suit the lofty theme.

The mock-epic (or mock-heroic) uses the epic structure but on a miniature scale. Its purpose is to ridicule a subject by describing events and emotions in an inflated heroic style so causing laughter through the inappropriateness. A later example of the mock-heroic is *The Rape of the Lock* in which the eighteenth-century poet Alexander Pope describes the 'theft' of a lock of hair as a matter of monumental importance. His aim was to reconcile two families who quarrelled as a result of this incident.

The fox's threat on Chauntecleer's life is similarly exaggerated in *The Nun's Priest's Tale*. The scholarly debate on the cause and interpretation of Chauntecleer's dream (116–390), the digression on free will versus predestination (464–85) and the dramatic account of Chauntecleer's fall (572–608) refer to many of the main theological and philosophical questions of Chaucer's day. (See Notes, pp. 67–9.) This is despite the reality that foxes eat hens. But we should not miss the ironic ambiguity. To a poor widow, the possible loss of a prize cockerel is nothing short of a catastrophe. The Nun's Priest tells us that when the fox is chased by the farmyard workers and their dogs, *It semed as that hevene sholde falle* (635). Is Chaucer exaggerating or telling the truth in this comparison?

The next activity asks you to look closely at the part of the tale which describes the reactions of Pertelote and the other hens when Chauntecleer is carried away by the fox. The allusions to the tragic events at Troy, Carthage and Rome are explained in the Notes, pp. 76–7. What you need to think about is why they are used here at the climax of the tale and with what effect.

Activity

- Read lines 589–607.
- With whom are the hens and Chauntecleer compared?
- What effect do the comparisons achieve?

Discussion

The classical points of reference suggest that Chauntecleer's fate is no less tragic than the death of King Priam of Troy, Hasdrubal or Roman senators at the burning of Rome. The mock-epic similes comparing Pertelote's shrieks with the lamentations of the grieving classical heroines for their heroes and husbands are comically incongruous when applied to a common farmyard happening.

The Nun's Priest is using the same rhetorical device of comparison that he used to introduce Chauntecleer at the beginning of the poem, but notice that Pertelote's cries are *Ful louder* (597) than those of the tragic women with whom she is compared. This is surely too much to take seriously, particularly as comparisons were encouraged by the rhetoricians provided that they were not so long that they detracted from the subject they were intended to embellish. Is The Nun's Priest admitting that three comparisons are excessive when he says, perhaps self-consciously, *Now wole I turne to my tale agayn* (608). One way of working out the effect of the comparisons is to try reading them out aloud to decide for yourself whether the lofty style is appropriate or absurdly out of place.

Realism

Although the predominant tone of the tale is mock-heroic, there are some very realistic touches. Realism or 'naturalism' was a relatively new style in Chaucer's time, often associated with the growing middle class who wanted entertainment that was not intellectually demanding. Unlike idealized courtly literature, it looked at life realistically and was often preoccupied with bodily functions of excretion and copulation. Realism is a key feature of a number of genres. One of the commonest is the *fabliau*, of which *The Miller's Tale* is a superbly bawdy example. What makes Chaucer an innovative poet in *The Nun's Priest's Tale* is the way in which he boldly mixes the courtly and realistic styles within the poem.

Activity

How successfully does Chaucer mix courtliness and realism in lines 385–96?

Discussion

Chauntecleer solemnly declares that his dream is a warning of dreadful events to come but it seems that even more terrifying to him is the thought of the *laxatyves* (196) which Pertelote has advised '*To purge you bynethe and eek above.*' (187). Notice how he slips from being authoritatively assertive to colloquially honest: '*I love hem never a deel!*' (390). Book learning and laxatives are both dismissed as he turns to his wife, *Madame Pertelote* (392), whose elevated courtly image is ironically deflated by the true-to-life description of the *scarlet reed aboute youre yen* (395). Chaucer makes us laugh by establishing a lofty ideal only to deflate it again. What is Chaucer's purpose? Is he mocking human pretension by telling us to accept life as it is rather than turn it into something it is not? Or is he simply being realistic himself in recognizing that the pilgrims would rather be entertained than preached at?

A similar shift from the noble ideal to everyday reality is seen at the beginning of the poem where the image of Chauntecleer as an aristocratic courtier (93–8) is almost immediately followed with the realism of a frightened cockerel who has had a bad dream (120–1).

The 'mixed style'

Much of the humour of the story of Chauntecleer and Pertelote comes from the way in which the story is told and how the different parts are put together. At first the tale may seem fragmented and confusing. It is best not to look for consistency so much as a series of overlapping viewpoints. The critic Muscatine uses the phrase 'mixed style' to describe Chaucer's writing because of its constantly changing focus (*Chaucer and the French Tradition*, p. 243). The challenge is in working out why

Chaucer chooses to tell the story of Chauntecleer and Pertelote through a mix of genres and stylistic shifts.

The Monk's Tale was monotonous and the host nearly fell asleep. In *The Nun's Priest's Tale* the 'mixed style' constantly challenges our expectations. The following activity asks you to look at the opening passage to see how the technique works.

Activity

Read lines 55–115.
- How is the *povre wydwe* (55) described in lines 55–80?
- How is Chauntecleer described in lines 81–115?
- What differences do you notice in the way in which the *povre wydwe* and Chauntecleer is each described?

Discussion

The widow who keeps Chauntecleer and the hens in *A yeerd... enclosed al aboute* (81) is carefully and realistically described. She is poor and humble. The Nun's Priest uses words like *pacience* (60) and *attempree* (72) to express his moral approval of her simplicity and self-sufficiency. She is not sufficiently important to be given a name at this point, neither does she speak. Why do you think this is? The Nun's Priest begins his story by soberly placing the cockerel in a farmyard with three cows, three pigs and a sheep.

When Chauntecleer is introduced it is as if a film changes from black and white to technicolour with full sound. The language of superlatives is used immediately, though significantly it is Chauntecleer's voice which is most impressive: *In al the land, of crowyng nas his peer* (84).

This is an accomplished cockerel who crows not by instinct but by astronomical calculation! The Nun's Priest follows the rhetorical rules – he has clearly read Geoffrey de Vinsauf (see Notes, pp. 37–8, and the section on Rhetoric, pp. 106) – and describes Chauntecleer from head to toe in rich, visual colours. Chauntecleer becomes a knight bearing a coat of arms, a richly-clad courtier and courtly lover of the *faire damoysele Pertelote* (104). A cockerel and the chosen one of seven hens become hero and heroine. This world of chivalry and romance is conveyed in the appropriate language of courtly culture – the hens are *paramours* (101) and Chauntecleer is a *gentil cok* (99).

But does Chaucer intend us to take this courtly love seriously?

There is a hint of laughter in the reference to the *Sevene hennes for to doon al his plesaunce* (100) where the tone slips sufficiently to remind us that the natural function of a cockerel is copulation, however it is described. And whilst we may be lulled into forgetting Chauntecleer's and Pertelote's avian role models, there is ample evidence that their colourful plumage is that of a real species of poultry. One of the effects of putting realism and courtliness side by side is to mock pretension but there are many other ways for the reader to respond.

If you read the description of The Prioress from the General Prologue (see Appendix, p. 159) you will note some marked contrasts between The Nun's Priest's employer and the poor widow. Perhaps The Nun's Priest deliberately begins his tale with the description of the widow to make sly digs at the worldliness of The Prioress as well as to mock the vanity of Chauntecleer. This is another example of Chaucer's ability to write on a number of levels simultaneously.

Structure, language and style

Narrative and narrators

All tales have tellers but *The Nun's Priest's Tale* is not a conventional narrative. Unlike the tellers of the other *Canterbury Tales*, we know almost nothing about the character of The Nun's Priest from the *General Prologue*, except that he was one of three priests to accompany The Prioress on the pilgrimage. However, there are aspects of the story which are in keeping with what might be expected from a man with his clerical background. He appears to be well read, knowledgeable about the Bible, history and the classics and aware of the contemporary theological and philosophical issues of debate.

In some respects, though, there are aspects of the story which are more characteristic of Chaucer's ironic viewpoint. In turn, much of the tale is told in the first person of Chauntecleer – three of his examples of prophetic dreams become fully-developed stories in their own right. In contrast to The Monk's tedious monologue, *The Nun's Priest's Tale* is almost a drama with the animated dialogue between Chauntecleer and Pertelote on the subject of love in the hen-coop and the cause of dreams, the suave flattery of Chauntecleer by the fox, and the narrator's commentary. Reading the tale aloud either on your own or in a group will help to convey the character of the person speaking.

Activity

One way to work out the identity of the different narrators is to divide the tale into different parts based on the voice of the person who is speaking. The following example has been begun for you but there is no absolutely correct or incorrect way of approaching this activity because many sections are interrelated. A possible structure is suggested below. It is up to you to decide for yourself where the voice and the tone of the story change.

Lines	Who is speaking and for what purpose?
1–54	Chaucer provides the *Prologue*, within which The Knight, The Host, The Monk and The Nun's Priest all speak.
55–122	The Nun's Priest describes the *povre wydwe* (55), Chauntecleer and Pertelote and introduces Chauntecleer's dream.
123–125	Pertelote complains about Chauntecleer's groaning.
126 –141	Chauntecleer gives an account of his dream.
142–203	Pertelote explains the dream's cause.
204–217	Chauntecleer states his belief in dreams.
218–296	Chauntecleer provides his first *exemplum* of a prophetic dream from an author he has read.
297–338	Chauntecleer provides a second *exemplum* which he claims to be by the same author.
339–343	Chauntecleer lectures Pertelote.
344–355	Chauntecleer provides a third *exemplum* (this time from the legend of St Kenelm).
356–390	Chauntecleer provides a list of *exempla* to impress Pertelote.
391–405	
406–420	
etc.	

Discussion

After Chauntecleer has proved his point, he turns to flattery and love talk (391–405) thereby forgetting that *dremes been significaciouns* (213). The Nun's Priest then resumes the narrative describing Chauntecleer's farmyard antics, and leading us into the next stage of the cockerel's *aventure* (420). We have to wait, however, while The Nun's Priest sets the date and time and describes Chauntecleer's happiness despite impending doom, *For evere the latter ende of joye is wo* (439) before he returns to his *sentence* (448).

The arrival of the fox (449–59) is almost immediately glossed with rhetorical commentary (460–500) by The Nun's Priest on treachery, predestination, free will and how *Wommannes conseil broghte us first to wo* (491). The actual story starts again on line 501 and develops with pace, with the fox's own voice flattering Chauntecleer (518–55), until line 559 when The Nun's Priest embellishes the story with rhetorical allusions to underline the seriousness of the situation. From line 609 to 635 the vivid description of the chase, albeit told by The Nun's Priest, has a life and momentum of its own and the narrator intervenes only briefly with a detached pointer, *Lo, how Fortune turneth sodeynly/The hope and pryde eek of hir enemy!* (637–8) before allowing the trickery and resolution to be dramatized through the voices of Chauntecleer and his enemy (641–69). The Nun's Priest concludes the tale not so much with a moral but an invitation to us to decide for ourselves what it means, and The Host provides the congratulatory *Epilogue* (681–96). (See Interpretations, p. 123.)

When the tale is read aloud, as it would have been dramatically told on the fictional pilgrimage, the layers of fiction become clearer as do the individual voices of the characters. Helen Cooper describes this structure of fictionality as working like a series of Russian dolls (*The Canterbury Tales*, Oxford Guides to Chaucer, second edition, pp. 347–48). On the outside is the poet Chaucer, who tells a story about his fictional self on the pilgrimage, who is recording a story told by the created character of The Nun's Priest. The Nun's Priest's story is about a cockerel, Chauntecleer, who recounts stories told him by people who have had dreams which have come true. The kaleidoscope of stories in *The Nun's Priest's Tale* is like the story collection of *The Canterbury Tales* in miniature, and just as styles between the separate *Canterbury Tales* are many and various, so within *The Nun's Priest's Tale* there are constant shifts in style as the focus and viewpoint of the narrators change. Given the complexity of the storytelling it is hardly surprising that we become more interested in *the chaf* (677) – the husk of the story – than *the fruyt* (677) – its core. (See Notes, pp. 82–3.)

The Host poses the fictional narrator – The Nun's Priest – with something of a problem. He is charged with the task of telling a story with a happy ending and *But I be myrie, ywis I wol be blamed* (51), but for many medieval clerics, the use of fables for teaching was frowned upon; too often the story carrying the moral became secular to the point that the religious teaching assumed a less than prominent place and *myrthe* (*General Prologue*, [766]) overtook *doctrine* (676). Perhaps it is for this reason that The Nun's Priest anticipates objections to his tale by reminding us of St Paul's belief that,

> ...al that writen is,
> To oure doctrine it is ywrite, ywis;   (675–6)

meaning 'For whatever is written was written for our instruction'.

It is not entirely clear whether Chaucer invents the persona of The Nun's Priest as a genuinely incompetent storyteller who unquestioningly adopts all the rules of rhetoric in order to hide his incompetence or whether The Nun's Priest knows exactly what he is doing but fakes incompetence to provoke laughter. Either way, it does not really matter because the overall effect is the same – an excellent story told in such an elaborately exaggerated fashion that we laugh as much at the telling as at the teller. If the mock-seriousness of an indiscriminate use of rhetorical skills serves as a cover for The Nun's Priest, it also makes us laugh at Chauntecleer's pretension.

Both The Nun's Priest and Chauntecleer misapply their learning though with different purposes and effects. But

Chaucer, through the fictional counterpart of The Nun's Priest, can present his ironic and humane understanding of human experience. As the critic Muscatine warns in his book *Chaucer and the French Tradition*, page 238:

> The tale will betray with laughter any too solemn scrutiny of its naked argument; if it is true that Chauntecleer and Pertelote are rounded characters, it is also true that they are chickens... Unlike fable *The Nun's Priest's Tale* does not so much make true and solemn assertions about life as it tests truths and tries out solemnities. If you are not careful, it will try out your solemnity too...

Rhetoric

Rhetoric is the art of effective or persuasive speaking or writing. (See Notes, pp. 37–9.) In the Middle Ages handbooks were written explaining how stylistic devices could be used to amplify or embellish material to effect. Chaucer is undoubtedly drawing on the instruction of such manuals in *The Nun's Priest's Tale* though he, himself, is too accomplished a writer to adopt the elaborate rules of rhetoric for their own sake. The activities below focus on some of the rhetorical features used – and parodied – by Chaucer.

It seems that there are two questions to ask: is rhetoric used deliberately inappropriately to make us laugh at the absurdity of lofty ideals in the farmyard, or is The Nun's Priest an incompetent storyteller using rhetoric he cannot control? These questions are worth thinking about as you consider how the various rhetorical devices are used.

Description and comparisons

Description was one of the more common rhetorical features for which instruction was given. In his *Poetria nova*, Geoffrey de Vinsauf offered this advice:

If description is to be the food and ample refreshment of the mind, avoid too curt a brevity... If you wish to describe, in amplified form, a woman's beauty:

Let the compass of Nature first fashion a sphere for her head; let the colour of gold give a glow to her hair, and lilies bloom high on her brow. Let her eyebrows resemble in dark beauty the blackberry, and a lovely and milk-white path separate their twin arches. Let her nose be straight, of moderate length, not too long nor too short for perfection. Let her eyes, those watch-fires of her brow, be radiant with emerald light, or with the brightness of stars. Let her countenance emulate dawn: not red, nor yet white – but at once neither of these colours and both. Let her mouth be bright, small in shape – as it were, a half-circle. Let her lips be rounded and full, but moderately so; let them glow, aflame, but with gentle fire. Let her teeth be snowy, regular, all of one size, and her breath like the fragrance of incense. Smoother than polished marble let Nature fashion her chin. Let her neck be a precious column of milk-white beauty, holding high the perfection of her countenance...

So let the radiant description descend from the top of her head to her toe, and the whole be polished to perfection.

(*Chaucer, Sources and Backgrounds*, Robert P. Miller (ed.), p. 67.)

Activity

Look at lines 81–98, where The Nun's Priest first describes Chauntecleer.
- Identify where Chaucer uses the rhetorical techniques of (a) comparison and (b) description.
- What is the effect of using these techniques?

Discussion

This is an impressive cockerel – almost a farmyard Pavarotti – best at crowing (84), tunefulness (85) and timing (87). Notice too the hint of secular pride as Chauntecleer surpasses the church organ and abbey clock with his vocal accomplishments.

Each of his avian parts is described from head to toe. The colours of *coral* (93), *jeet* (95) and *asure* (96) suggest that

Chauntecleer is like a knight in heraldic colours, a priest, perhaps, in rich vestments, a carefully groomed lover with *nayles whitter than the lylye flour* (97). By association he becomes rich, protective and chivalrous.

Circumlocution

Another technique of rhetoric is *circumlocutio* or circumlocution – talking around the point to sound impressive. A typical example is in lines 157–73 where Pertelote gives a point for point analysis of Chauntecleer's dream according to the theory of humours (see Notes, pp. 47–8). In context, her use of rhetoric is appropriate: she wants to impress Chauntecleer with her learning so that he will do as she tells him. However, it is harder for us to take seriously a hen's use of rhetorical language, even if Chauntecleer does.

Activity

Look at lines 421–31.
- How does The Nun's Priest use circumlocution to describe the day of Chauntecleer's seizure by the fox?
- What is the effect of using this stylistic technique?

Discussion

The joke is not so much what The Nun's Priest is saying but the way that he says it. The long-winded and complicated use of astrological reference to tell the time gives a mock-solemnity to the events which follow but also mocks the seriousness of medieval astrologers, whose calculations are imitated – and parodied – here. The Nun's Priest takes 11 lines to say that this part of the story begins at 9 a.m. on 3 May. (See Notes to lines 428–9, p. 63.)

The length of the passage is a means of moving from the discussion of dreams to the main plot, but it also delays the telling of Chauntecleer's *aventure* (420). It is as though The Nun's Priest is tantalizing the audience by pretending to get to the plot and then moving away from it. On the one hand, the device of circumlocution increases the suspense but, on the other, the complicated calculation of the date of that fateful day is a frustrating distraction.

Digressions

As the Notes remind us (p. 62–3) and as you may have discovered in tracking the plot (see p. 95) there is more commentary and amplification than action in *The Nun's Priest's Tale*. Digressions were part of a medieval rhetorician's art. They allowed him to support his argument with examples as well as to display his learning through allusions. They were, however, only encouraged if they developed a point relevantly!

Activity

Look at what The Nun's Priest says about free will and predestination in lines 464–84.

• What is the effect of this digression at this point in the tale?

Discussion

This digression exemplifies rhetorical *circumlocutio* and, in part, the rhetorical figure of *occupatio*, that is, saying you will not say something while actually outlining the main points. The complex argument about free will and predestination is explained in the Notes (p. 00). To summarize: The Nun's Priest is saying that he is not sure whether one's fate is predestined by God, *by necessitee* (479) – in which case one can do nothing about it – or whether one has *free choys* (480) to determine one's own destiny. A third position, in this theological argument, is that God's foreknowledge constrains but does not exclude freedom of action (483–4).

So, just as the fox is *Waitynge his tyme on Chauntecleer to falle* (457), The Nun's Priest digresses to consider whether Chauntecleer's fall is predestined by God, *by necessitee* (479), or whether God gave Chauntecleer *free choys* (480), to take heed of the dream's warning or to ignore it. This intellectual debate, which was to split medieval Christendom, is transposed to the farmyard. Here Chaucer certainly seems to be mocking the medieval theologians in applying their serious theological arguments to birds. The effect of this, as of many of the other digressions, is to enhance the mock-heroic tone. After all, foxes regularly eat chickens. This is a fact of life rather than a subject for profound theological debate.

Exclamation or apostrophe

Some of the more immediately obvious rhetorical devices are the exclamations (*exclamatio*), also known as apostrophes. The following lines, which break across the now fast-moving story at the point where the fox is lurking in the cabbages, use apostrophe (or exclamation) to comic effect.

> O false mordrour, lurkynge in thy den!
> O newe Scariot, newe Genylon,
> False dissymulour, o Greek Synon,
> That broghtest Troye al outrely to sorwe!   (460–3)

Daun Russell (568), the fox, is identified as no less a traitor than Judas Iscariot, Ganelon, and Sinon, who betrayed Christ, Charlemagne, and the Trojans respectively. The irony is implicit because you have to decide for yourself whether the narrator is serious or not in suggesting that the fox's naturally predatory instinct is comparable with some of the greatest betrayals in history.

Ideas and themes

Dreams

The question whether dreams tell the truth would have been as topical for Chaucer's pilgrims as astrology is today. Almost half the tale is given to Chauntecleer's dream and the debate about its meaning. Chauntecleer himself cites Macrobius, a fifth-century authority on dreams (357). Very simply, Macrobius classifies dreams into five types. The first three are prophetic: the *somnium*, which foretells the future in an allegorical way, that is, where one thing stands for another; the *visio*, which is a straightforward vision of the future; and the *oraculum*, where a person appears to the dreamer, prophesies the future and offers advice. Chauntecleer is certain that his destiny has been revealed to him in a *somnium*. The other two kinds of dream, the *insomnium*, or nightmare, and the *phantasma*, are not prophetic in any way and can be caused by mental anxiety or physical distress, for example, indigestion. Pertelote thinks that Chauntecleer's dream is one of these meaningless nightmares. Chaucer himself acknowledges the complex arguments about the meaning of dreams in the opening lines of *The House of Fame* (1–52) where his amused and bemused summary perhaps also typifies his attitude to the debate.

Activity

Read lines 116–41.
- How does Chauntecleer react to his dream?
- What does his reaction show about his character?

Discussion

In keeping with the philosophers he admires, Chauntecleer is sure that his dawn dream is prophetic and is *soore afright* (129). However, we do not need to be medieval philosophers to know that the normal behaviour of animals and birds is to react instinctively and fearfully to predators. (See Notes, p. 46.)

Are we supposed to take Chauntecleer's fear seriously? One approach is to ask if we are in any doubt as to the object of Chauntecleer's dream – the *beest* which *Was lyk an hound* and which *was bitwixe yelow and reed* (133–9). From the beginning the audience has the advantage of Chauntecleer. On the one hand we laugh at the absurd vanity of a cockerel trying to prove that, like Scipio, Daniel, Joseph, Croesus, Hector and others, his tragic destiny has been revealed to him in a dream; on the other hand, with the benefit of experience we know that foxes frequently eat hens. By applying scholarly interpretations of dreams to a cockerel and hen, is Chaucer mocking Chauntecleer's self-importance or the pedantry of medieval philosophers?

The next section of the poem (142–390) follows the form of a learned disputation. The domestic argument between Chauntecleer and Pertelote is a parody – a comic equivalent – of the great debate between philosophers and medieval doctors on the meaning and causes of dreams.

Pertelote is in no doubt that Chauntecleer's dream is *vanitee* (156) – a dream with no meaning. She supports her view with a carefully argued exposition on medieval medicine (155–203). (See Notes, pp. 47–8.) She then urges a rather less carefully considered remedy for the imbalance of *colera* (162) and *malencolie* (167) that she diagnoses as the dream's cause. She cites Cato as an authority to give weight to her argument.

In the manner of disputation, Chauntecleer takes up her reference to Cato as a means of opening the counter-argument *That dremes been significaciouns* (213) according to *many a man moore of auctorite* (209). His refutation is impressive: three examples – or *exempla* – to illustrate his point, together with a wealth of learned allusions to reinforce his forceful argument that it is folly to ignore dreams' warnings.

To call it a debate is possibly an exaggeration. Do Chauntecleer or Pertelote change their minds as a result? There is less of the cut and thrust of a real debate than one-sided assertion. It seems that, as in many domestic arguments, the minds of husband and wife were made up from the outset.

Activity
Read lines 142–203.
- What does the debate on dreams tell us about the character of Pertelote?

Discussion
Pertelote seems less horrified by Chauntecleer's fears than by his apparent cowardice: *'Have ye no mannes herte, and han a berd?'* (154). When she ascribes the cause to an imbalance of humours (159–73) (see Notes, pp. 47–8) she reveals her essentially practical, homely nature by suggesting that Chauntecleer's premonition of

danger may be caused by nothing more than indigestion. She also knows that her husband will be more impressed by scholarly reference than by common sense. Her knowledge of medieval science is pedantically displayed in a point-for-point analysis of the effect of a superfluity of *colera* (162) and *malencolie* (167) and the proposed cure is no less thorough. But in the absence of an apothecary, she will prescribe a homemade concoction of laxatives, '*To purge yow bynethe and eek above.*' (187).

Are we to take this as an impressive display of medieval medical knowledge or is Chaucer deliberately satirizing learning? Pertelote's proposed herbal remedy sounds like a deadly brew and one that might have proved fatal by itself had Chauntecleer been brave enough to do as he was told. Pertelote's advice is well intended but sometimes short-sighted. Notice that she even advises the cockerel to avoid dawn! (See Note to line 189, p. 50.)

> 'Ware the sonne in his ascencioun
> Ne fynde yow nat repleet of humours hoote.' (190–1)

It is hardly surprising that Chauntecleer tries to outdo his wife in mustering all the scholarly, rhetorical skills he can to refute her argument. She only cited one authority, Cato, to support her case; Chauntecleer provides two fully developed illustrative *exempla* (218–96, and 301–38) each of which he embellishes far beyond the original to become stories in their own right. In fact, the storytelling is so overdone, you may be lulled, like Chauntecleer, into forgetting the point they are intended to reinforce.

Chauntecleer's ability to cite authorities is remarkable for a cockerel. He has no problem in linking his fate with some of the greatest tragedies ever told. Such is his pride that he is in no doubt that his dream prophesies disaster of similar proportions.

It is easy to forget that this is a cockerel and hen speaking, because their intellectual pretensions are so typical of human behaviour. Does Chauntecleer really believe his own arguments or are they a means of concealing his own fears from himself, and his cowardice from his wife, by 'pulling the feathers' over his own and Pertelote's eyes? This is a very human cockerel – a courtier, a lover and a scholar – with a very convincing psychology. Chauntecleer claims to have had his tragic destiny revealed to him in his dream but is he using his argument to bolster his masculine pride or to conceal his cowardice? Notice that Chaucer makes no judgement; he leaves that to us:

> 'Shortly I seye, as for conclusioun,
> That I shat han of this avisioun
> Adversitee; and I seye forthermoor
> That I ne telle of laxatyves no stoor,
> For they been venymes, I woot it weel;
> I hem diffye, I love hem never a deel!'   (385–90)

Attitudes to women

As you have seen, Chaucer frequently adapted well-known stories and styles for his own purposes. Elsewhere in *The Canterbury Tales*, he presented the reader with male and female characters who did not conform to traditional role models. In many of the tales, the subject is mastery in love, desire and marriage. The use of the fable in *The Nun's Priest's Tale* enables Chaucer to indulge his fascination with human behaviour and relationships through a cock and hen story. But as we have seen before, the boundary between the birds and humans is thinly drawn. Chauntecleer and Pertelote's relationship is psychologically plausible as humans and birds simultaneously so that our response depends upon how much of ourselves we recognize behind the plumage.

Look at the introduction of Chauntecleer and Pertelote:

> This gentil cok hadde in his governaunce
> Sevene hennes for to doon al his plesaunce...
> Of whiche the faireste hewed on hir throte
> Was cleped faire damoysele Pertelote.
> Curteys she was, discreet, and debonaire,

And compaignable, and bar hyrself so faire
Syn thilke day that she was seven nyght oold
That trewely she hath the herte in hoold
Of Chauntecleer, loken in every lith; (99–109)

Chauntecleer is a noble, *gentil* (99) cockerel (see Note to line 99, p. 44 for the meaning of *gentil*); Pertelote is raised to the level of courtliness with the French *faire damoysele* (104) and has many of the qualities of a courtly lady, *Curteys she was, discreet, and debonaire* (105). She is the romantic heroine, and Chauntecleer is her courtly lover. She holds his heart and he worships and serves her. However, the reference to the *Sevene hennes for to doon al his plesaunce* (100) is a reminder that, for a cockerel, a courtly relationship is a contradiction in terms. A cockerel's function is to serve all the hens even though it is the *faire* (104) Pertelote who is chosen to share his frustratingly narrow perch in the *halle* (118). Perhaps Chaucer is also hinting at the reality of sexual desire lurking behind the pure image of courtly love?

Overtones of sexual vigour and pleasure remind us of both the farmyard and human reality though the ironic ambiguity minimizes any offence to the pilgrims. If they see anything in Chauntecleer's behaviour that is applicable to the human condition, it is not because of what Chaucer, or The Nun's Priest, has said.

The idealized roles are difficult to keep up. When Chauntecleer has his dream, his heroic valour evaporates and though he tries to keep his dignity by asserting that, like the heroes he cites, he has been given a glimpse of his destiny, there is no disguising his fear of both the *beest* (133) of his dream and the laxatives Pertelote prescribes for the cure. Similarly the *faire* (104) Pertelote is essentially practical when she reacts to Chauntecleer's groaning.

Activity

Read lines 142–203.
- How is Pertelote portrayed?
- Is her response romantic or realistic?

Discussion

Pertelote first responds to Chauntecleer's fears as the romantic heroine accusing Chauntecleer of cowardice:

> 'Now han ye lost myn herte and al my love!
> I kan nat love a coward, by my feith!'　　　　(144–5)

before resorting to the self-righteous warning of the practical wife about what will happen if he takes no notice of her advice:

> '...I dar wel leye a grote,
> That ye shul have a fevere terciane,
> Or an agu that may be youre bane.'　　　　(192–4)

Is she suggesting that if there's one thing worse than living with a cowardly lover, it is having to cope with an ailing husband? Pertelote's reaction to Chauntecleer's dream is essentially practical and earthly. Though she is knowledgeable about the causes of dreams and their remedies, she uses her learning to deflate Chauntecleer's egoism. Chaucer seems to be exploring the universal theme of the roles that men and women (cocks and hens) have thrust upon them.

Jill Mann, in her book *Geoffrey Chaucer*, pages 187–9, sums up the modern relevance of the human situation neatly:

> It is the episode of Chauntecleer's dream in particular that
> shows the construction of gender differences by representing
> them as pressures exerted by each sex on the other...
> Chauntecleer has masculinity thrust upon him. And this is a fair
> exchange for the imposition of delicate femininity on *faire
> damoysele Pertelote*. The pressure on women to conform to an
> image of meek and gentle femininity inevitably translates itself
> into a pressure on men to be brave and strong.
>
> 　　...Pertelote fuels the myth of masculine bravado in the same

way, talking away her husband's cowardice by insisting that his bad dream is merely a product of indigestion, and must be dosed away with laxatives. The graceful serenity of the romantic heroine is sustained by the desperate underwater paddling of domestic nagging (176–84).

The cock is as eager to preserve his masculine dignity as is his wife, but he is equally eager to avoid taking any laxatives. He therefore resorts to a learned demonstration of the importance of dreams, as a way of achieving both ends at the same time. Female practicality is pounded into submission by the heavy guns of masculine rhetoric, relentlessly reiterating the same point, that *dremes been to drede* (297). It is only when this imposing rhetorical edifice is complete that the undignified nature of its foundation – the cock's hatred of the *venymes* laxatives become clear (387–90). Chauntecleer's last *ensample*, Hector's dismissal of his wife Andromache's premonitory dream of his death (375–82), ironically reflects his own masculine resistance to female interference.

Relationships between men and women

The relationship between the sexes is presented with superb irony. Chauntecleer's patronizing attitude towards Pertelote is unmistakable. She cites Cato as her authority but Chauntecleer assembles so many other authorities to support his case that his pedantic display of scholarly superiority does not allow Pertelote to get a squawk in edgeways. In addition he attempts to smooth her feathers by addressing her as '*Dame Pertelote*' (356) and '*Madame*' (204), condescendingly implying that he knows what he is talking about and she doesn't. Do you think that Pertelote is impressed by Chauntecleer's learning and is fooled by his arrogance? Does her silence show docile submission or female shrewdness?

Chauntecleer uses flattery, together with the traditional compliment to his mistress's eyes (albeit henlike) to change the subject:

> For whan I se the beautee of youre face,
> Ye been so scarlet reed aboute youre yen,
> It maketh al my drede for to dyen; (394–6)

Chauntecleer is not the first male to have his confidence restored through sexual gratification (411–15). Copulating with Pertelote makes scholarly disputation on the significance of dreams irrelevant (404–05). The irony is that Chauntecleer has reinforced his belief in dreams through three *exempla* and a host of rhetorical references only to abandon the wisdom of his own learning when something more pleasurable comes along.

What makes his behaviour even more humorous is his misuse of the Latin tag '*Mulier est hominis confusio*' (398) to justify his behaviour. (See Notes, pp. 61–2.)

Activity

> 'For al so siker as *In principio,*
> *Mulier est hominis confusio* –
> Madame, the sentence of this Latyn is,
> "Womman is mannes joye and al his blis."' (397–400)

- What do these lines tell us about Chauntecleer?
- Why are they ironic?

You may find it useful to refer to the Notes, pp. 61–2.

Discussion

These four lines tell us a lot about Chauntecleer's character. He flatters Pertelote, gently suggesting that as his lady she is the cause of his happiness. Given the choice between love-making or medicine to cure his ills, it is difficult to know whether Chauntecleer's words are amorous foreplay or a deliberate ploy to make her forget the laxatives. In the event, he achieves both objectives.

Does Chauntecleer deliberately mistranslate the Latin tag '*Mulier est hominis confusio*' (398)? Chauntecleer tells Pertelote it means '*Womman is mannes joye and al his blis*' (400), but the accurate translation is 'Woman is man's ruin'. Do you think he is having a joke at Pertelote's expense or is he revealing his ignorance? Chaucer carefully leaves the question open to debate.

Nonetheless, Chauntecleer's love-making with Pertelote is his ruin. Having reasserted his manliness by 'feathering' her, he has conveniently forgotten the warning of his dream. Ironically, because Pertelote is his bliss, she is also his undoing.

Both Chaucer and The Nun's Priest neatly side-step making a judgement on women. Chaucer seldom makes explicit judgements in his poetry, preferring to allow the reader to draw independent conclusions. The Nun's Priest similarly refuses to be drawn openly into the argument, though possibly for different reasons. His superior is, after all, The Prioress, on whose favour his employment depends and there are women such as The Wife of Bath among the pilgrims whom he would be wise not to offend.

Activity

- Look carefully at the attitudes to women in lines 486–500.
- What do you think is The Nun's Priest's view of women?

Discussion

These lines typify The Nun's Priest's ambivalent attitude. At first, it seems that there is a harsh criticism of women. By association, Pertelote's *wommennes conseils* (490) are equated with Eve's part in the downfall of man, a comparison which is perhaps a little far-fetched when applied to a domestic disagreement in the farmyard. The Nun's Priest retracts the suggestion, however, almost as soon as it is made, claiming that he has no wish to offend the audience. He says he is only joking and that he is only repeating the cock's words, ironically concluding, *I kan noon harm of no womman divyne* (500).

On closer exploration of this passage, The Nun's Priest is seen to be distorting the truth. Chauntecleer did not *take conseil of his wyf* (487) – he fiercely, and at length, argued that dreams foretold the future. When Chauntecleer walks in the yard that morning it is because he wants to exert his masculinity and exhibit his macho behaviour for all to see. This is why he is heedless of his own beliefs, not because of anything Pertelote has said.

You could compare your response to this passage with Jill Mann's interpretation:

> Chaucer's Chauntecleer fails to internalize his own arguments on dreams, for the very good reason – as we have seen – they were generated only by his desire to avoid taking laxatives. The same interpretative facility with which the cock so successfully fended off the medicinal dose is here set to work by the teller of the tale to conjure up a male alibi out of the ready store of anti-feminist clichés, with a sublime indifference to the facts of the case.   (*Geoffrey Chaucer*, p. 193)

Chaucer yet again shows his ability to explore a universal theme through the particulars of Chauntecleer's and Pertelote's relationship. His presentation of this battle between the sexes would seem to be as relevant now as it was then.

Taketh the moralite...

Many medieval preachers traditionally used fables as *exempla*, or examples, to illustrate a moral point (see Notes, p. 37) and therefore it is not surprising that in drawing his tale to a close that The Nun's Priest invites his audience to consider its moral teaching: *Taketh the moralite, goode men* (674). But whereas Chauntecleer used the stories of the man in the dung-cart and the sea travellers as *exempla* to reinforce his argument that dreams foretold the future, The Nun's Priest's reason for telling the story of Chauntecleer and Pertelote is less immediately clear and the tale has a number of possible moral interpretations. (See Notes, pp. 79–8.)

Activity
- Read carefully lines 663–71.
- What moral points are made?
- How fitting are they as a conclusion to the tale?

Discussion

After the double trick in which the fox persuades Chauntecleer to close his eyes and open his mouth and Chauntecleer in turn tricks the fox into opening his mouth and closing his eyes, metaphorically speaking, each draws his own moral conclusion.

Chauntecleer refuses to be tricked twice and says to the fox:

> 'Thou shalt namoore thurgh thy flaterye
> Do me to synge and wynke with myn ye;
> For he that wynketh, whan he sholde see,
> Al wilfully, God lat him nevere thee!'   (663–6)

And the fox replies:

> '... but God yeve hym meschaunce,
> That is so undiscreet of governaunce
> That jangleth whan he sholde holde his pees.'   (667–9)

And The Nun's Priest points the moral:

> Lo, swich it is for to be recchelees
> And necligent, and truste on flaterye.   (670–1)

It is characteristically plausible that Chauntecleer's voice – *In al the land, of crowyng nas his peer* (84) – should be the cause of his downfall, and that *So was he ravysshed with his flaterie* (558), Chauntecleer fails to see the irony of the fox's claim that he knew his father (529–31). Chauntecleer opens his mouth to show off his singing; the fox opens his mouth to boast of his capture of the cockerel. Both are complacently blind as not to see what is happening, literally or metaphorically, though Chauntecleer is sufficiently quick-witted to escape by using the very trick of flattery through which he was caught.

Chauntecleer's vanity and complacency both contribute to his downfall. He is an easy victim of flattery, not recognizing the much-vaunted foe of his dream when he meets him face to face, suggesting that experience is a better teacher than book-learning. (Ironically, this is what he had claimed earlier in lines 216–17.) Only after his fortunate escape from the jaws of death does he admit the error of complacency, of *he that wynketh, whan he sholde see* (665). The fox likewise learns belatedly that boasting has lost him a meal because he *jangleth whan he sholde holde his pees* (669). The Nun's Priest's moralizing statement,

> Lo, swich it is for to be recchelees
> And necligent, and truste on flaterye.   (670–1)

applies equally to both bird and beast as well as to his audience to whom it is also directed.

Activity

- Read lines 670–80.
- What do you think these lines mean?

Discussion

Certainly the many morals offered at the end of *The Nun's Priest's Tale* suggest that there is no definitive reading of the morality of the tale. The alternatives are discussed fully in the Notes (see pp. 79–80) but it is also possible that The Nun's Priest – and Chaucer – are mocking our expectation that a fable must have a moral. Though it is The Nun's Priest who asks his audience to consider the *moralite* (674), and in fact ends the tale in a style befitting the end of a sermon (678–80), Chaucer's and The Nun's Priest's voices merge (670–80) in challenging us to sort out *the fruyt* from *the chaf* (677).

   Is the invitation *Taketh the moralite* (674) to be taken seriously or ironically? Some critics see this passage as the conventional conclusion to an exemplary fable; others think it pokes fun at, or subverts, the genre. In *The Nun's Priest's Tale* there are many examples of statements which are made seriously – or with mock-seriousness – which are later laughed at. For example, The Nun's Priest suggests *Wommennes conseils been ful ofte colde* (490) only to claim that he was joking, *I seyde it in my game* (496) and *Thise been the cokkes wordes, and nat myne;/I kan noon harm of no womman divyne* (499–500). This technique is typical of Chaucer's irony in putting forward ideas but leaving judgement to the reader.

There is, however, another way to read this passage, put forward by Alfred David in *The Strumpet Muse*, pages 229–30.

> This passage... has been treated as... an open invitation to read not only *The Nun's Priest's Tale* but all of Chaucer's works as allegories in which we must search for the fruit of sentence beneath the chaff of fiction... There is another way of looking at the *moralite* of the tale. The main target of the satire seems to be precisely the tendency to look for a moral everywhere, to peck up the kernels of sentence *and ete hem yn*... If the tale is a satire on pride, then it is surely on pride in our human intelligence.

Perhaps we should take heed of the warning at the end of *The Miller's Prologue* that *men shal nat maken ernest of game* (*The Miller's Tale*, [78]), and not take a joke too seriously!

The Epilogue

In *The Nun's Priest's Prologue*, The Host had challenged The Nun's Priest to *Be blithe* (46) and make *hertes glade* (45). The Nun's Priest seems to have succeeded, judging by the fulsome approval of The Host, whose lewd outburst at the end of the tale, '*I-blessed be thy breche, and every stoon!*' (682) sets the tone of *The Epilogue*. Perhaps his blessing of The Nun's Priest's buttocks and testicles says more about The Host than about The Nun's Priest? Certainly The Host does not concern himself with *moralite* (674)!

Traditionally, it has been customary for readers of *The Canterbury Tales* to make some judgement about the match of tale to teller. As discussed earlier (see Notes, p. 29 and Interpretations, p. 87), this is almost impossible with *The Nun's Priest's Tale* when so little is known about The Nun's Priest. The Host responds not by linking the subject matter of this moral fable with its narrator, but through hinting at an element of wish-fulfilment in The Nun's Priest's portrayal of Chauntecleer. He seizes on the birdlike appearance of The Nun's Priest with

> 'So gret a nekke, and swich a large breest!
> He loketh as a sperhauk with his yen;'　　　　　　　(690–1)

to support his belief that the teller would be *a trede-foul aright* (685), possibly in *nede of hennes, .../Ya, moo than seven tymes seventenen* (687–8), if he were not a priest. Do you think that The Host is making lewd digs about the sexual frustrations of celibate priests in general or sly suggestions about the sexual desire of The Nun's Priest in particular? Either way, in congratulating The Nun's Priest on his *murie tale* (683), The Host exploits the popular topic of priests and sex. Behind The Host's words though, we can also detect Chaucer's characteristic irony in suggesting that there may be a difference between how people might be expected or wish to behave and how they actually do.

Significantly, The Nun's Priest makes no reply and *The Epilogue* is as enigmatic as the ending of the tale itself. Chaucer may be preparing the reader for the debate on sex found in other tales but, at the end of *The Nun's Priest's Tale* he leaves us to draw our own conclusions about its meaning and its teller on the basis of the evidence of the tale and our understanding of human behaviour.

Critical views

Critics have taken various views of *The Nun's Priest's Tale*, some of which have been referred to previously. The following are some other interpretations of the tale for you to consider.

Some critics have seen the whole poem as an allegory of the Fall of man through pride. (In allegory, abstract or moral ideas are represented by people – or as in this case by birds and beasts.) Chauntecleer, like Adam, is tempted by the fox, representing the snake in the garden of Eden, or the devil, and the confusion of the farmyard chase following his fall is a burlesque on the universal chaos and moral disorder following the Fall of man.

These views are usually supported by the biblical references within the poem which are explained in the Notes. Alternatively you might argue that the biblical and doctrinal references contribute to the mock-heroic elevation of Chauntecleer to a level comically inappropriate for a cockerel but detract from the humour if taken too literally.

Other critics have seen Chauntecleer's flaw as male vanity, and the triumph of passion over reason – copulating with Pertelote rather than heeding the warning of his dream – as responsible for his downfall. Chauntecleer's sexual psychology and human behaviour have much in common.

A further group of critics has seen the poem as The Nun's Priest's thinly disguised anti-feminist jibes at the social niceties of his superior, The Prioress, or his disapproval of the worldliness of The Monk, though such interpretations owe more to speculative inference than to real evidence.

A final word of warning, however, about considering the views of the critics... if we are not careful, the more serious we become, the more we shall sound like Chauntecleer.

Essay Questions

1   Is the purpose of *The Nun's Priest's Tale* to teach or to delight?

2   How successfully does Chaucer integrate courtly love and sex into *The Nun's Priest's Tale*?

3   *'My tale is of a cok'*, says The Nun's Priest. John Speirs says that 'The Nun's Priest's Tale *illustrates some central truths about human nature with subtle irony and humane wisdom'* (John Speirs, *Chaucer the Maker*). With which of these statements do you agree? Use detailed evidence from *The Nun's Priest's Tale* to support your view.

4   Which stylistic features do you think Chaucer uses most effectively to create the characters of Chauntecleer and Pertelote? Describe these features with detailed reference to **three** or **four** passages from *The Nun's Priest's Tale* and explain the effect they create.

5   Consider the characters of Chauntecleer and Pertelote. In this battle between the sexes, who do you think wins and why?

6   *'Telle us swich thyng as may oure hertes glade'*, says the Host to The Nun's Priest. How successfully do you think The Nun's Priest does as he is asked?

7   'In *The Nun's Priest's Tale*, Chaucer's attitude towards Chauntecleer and Pertelote is sympathetic rather than judgemental.' How far do you agree with this view?

8   With close reference to **three** or **four** passages in *The Nun's Priest's Tale*, identify some of the stylistic features of the mock-heroic and explain their effect in the poem.

9   How far does *The Nun's Priest's Tale* reflect the medieval idea
    of the Wheel of Fortune?

This thirteenth-century wall painting
from Rochester Cathedral illustrates
the widespread medieval idea of 'The
Wheel of Fortune'. The idea is that
Fortune's ever-turning wheel brings
people up to prosperity and then
dashes them down the other side to
calamity.

10 What is the function of dreams in *The Nun's Priest's
    Tale*? How does Chaucer link Chauntecleer's dream and the
    exemplary stories concerning dreams to the rest of the tale?

11 At the end of *The Nun's Priest's Tale*, The Nun's Priest invites his audience to 'Taketh the moralite' (674). With detailed reference to the poem, what do you think is the moral of *The Nun's Priest's Tale*?

12 What techniques does the fox use to beguile Chauntecleer? How does the temptation of Chauntecleer relate to the rest of the tale?

13 Which aspects of fourteenth-century society and its beliefs do you regard as most important in order to understand *The Nun's Priest's Tale*?

Chronology

1315–16   Great Famine

1321–2   Civil War in England

1327   Deposition and death of Edward II; accession of Edward III

1337   Start of the Hundred Years War

Early 1340s Geoffrey Chaucer born, the son of John (wine merchant) and Agnes – originally the family came from Ipswich

1346   Defeat of the French at Crécy

1348   Black Death

1350   Statute of Labourers' Act passed

1356–9   Chaucer becomes a page in the household of the Countess of Ulster

1359   Fought in the wars with France in the army of Prince Lionel

1360   Captured and ransomed

1360–6   Studied law and finance at The Inns of Court; 1361 second major occurrence of plague; 1362 *Piers Plowman* published

1366   Evidence of Chaucer travelling in Europe, possibly on a pilgrimage; married (Philippa); Chaucer's father died

1366–70   Chaucer travelled again to Europe, four times; destinations unknown but possibly including a journey to Italy; 1367 first record of Chaucer's membership of the royal household – a squire in the court

1368–72	*The Book of the Duchess* written in this period; before 1372 translated the *Roman de la Rose* (*The Romaunt of the Rose*)
1372–3	Chaucer on King's business in Italy
1374	Moved to Aldgate in London; appointed Customs Controller (to control taxes on wool, sheepskins, and leather)
1376–7	Further travelling in Flanders and France on King's secret business. In 1376 'Good Parliament' meets; death of Edward, the Black Prince. 1377 death of Edward III; accession of Richard II
1378	Travelled again to Italy – renewed acquaintance with works of Italian writers
1378–80	*The House of Fame* written; 1379 Richard II introduces Poll Tax
1380–2	*The Parliament of Fowls* written; 1381 Peasants' Revolt
1380s	Chaucer moved to Kent
1382–6	*Troilus and Criseyde* and *The Legend of Good Women* written; 1385 gave up the post at Customs House and became Justice of the Peace
1386	Gave up house at Aldgate; election to Parliament
1387	Philippa presumed to have died
1388–92	The *General Prologue* and earlier *Canterbury Tales* written; 1389–91 appointed Clerk of the King's Works. 1391–2 *A Treatise on the Astrolabe* written
1392–5	Most of *The Canterbury Tales* completed
1396–1400	Later *Canterbury Tales* written; 1396 Anglo-French Treaty. 1397–9 Richard II's reign of 'tyranny'

1399   Chaucer returned to London, living in a house
near the Lady Chapel of Westminster Abbey;
deposition of Richard II; accession of Henry IV

1400   Chaucer died (date on tomb on Westminster
Abbey given as 25 October)

Further Reading

Editions

This edition provides details of scholarship on the tale:
Derek Pearsall (ed.), 'The Nun's Priest's Tale' (University of
    Oklahoma Press, 1983, Volume II part 9 of *A Variorum
    Edition of the Works of Geoffrey Chaucer*.

These school editions have useful notes and glossaries:
N. Coghill and C. Tolkien (eds), *The Nun's Priest's Tale* (Harrap,
    1959).
M. Hussey (ed.), *The Nun's Priest's Prologue and Tale* (Cambridge
    University Press, 1965).
K. Sisam (ed.), *The Nun's Priest's Tale* (Oxford University Press,
    1927).

Criticism

This book provides a good commentary on the tale:
Piero Boitani and Jill Mann (eds), *The Cambridge Chaucer
    Companion* (Cambridge University Press, 1986).

This book in the series Oxford Guides to Chaucer describes
    issues and debates in recent criticism of the tale:
Helen Cooper, *The Canterbury Tales*, second edition (Oxford
    University Press, 1996).

This book looks at the relationship between form, meaning and
    style in the tale:
Helen Cooper, *The Structure of* The Canterbury Tales
    (Duckworth, 1983).

This book explores the tension between teaching and laughter in the tale:
A. David, *The Strumpet Muse* (Indiana University Press, 1976).

This article discusses the relationship between the tale and its historical context:
Richard W. Fehrenbacher, ' "A Yeerd Enclosed Al About": Literature and History in *The Nun's Priest's Tale*', *Chaucer Review* 29 (1994), pp. 134–48.

This article considers the features of sermons and preaching in the tale:
Susan Gallick, 'A Look at Chaucer and his Preachers', *Speculum* 50 (1975), pp. 456–76.

This article explores the significance of the widow's poverty in relation to the wealth of some of the clerical pilgrims:
Dinah Hazell, 'Poverty and Plenty: Chaucer's povre wydwe and her gentil cok', *Mediaevalia* 25 (2004), pp. 26–65.

This article discusses The Knight's function in *The Nun's Priest's Prologue*:
R. E. Kaske, 'The Knight's Interruption of *The Monk's Tale*', *English Literary History* 24 (1957), pp. 249–68.

This article describes the fable qualities of the tale, including rhetoric and morality:
R. T. Lenaghan, 'The Nun's Priest's Fable', *Publications of the Modern Language Association* 75 (1963), pp. 300–07.

This book provides a well-argued feminist reading:
J. Mann, *Geoffrey Chaucer* (Harvester, 1991).

This article considers the use of fables to preach and to entertain:
Stephen Manning, 'The Nun's Priest's Morality and the Medieval Attitude toward Fables', *Journal of English and Germanic Philology* 59 (1960), pp. 403–16.

This book provides a fine discussion of the style of the tale:
C. Muscatine, *Chaucer and the French Tradition* (University of
California, 1957).

This book provides a balanced and incisive account of the
issues of the tale:
D. Pearsall, *The Canterbury Tales* (Unwin, 1985).

Background information

This is an anthology of medieval writings about women:
Alcuin Blamires (ed.), *Woman Defamed and Woman Defended*
(Oxford University Press, 1992).

This book provides information on medieval theories about
medicine and dreams:
W. C. Curry, *Chaucer and the Medieval Sciences* (London, 1960).

This book provides an introduction to medieval ideas about
dreams:
C. S. Lewis, *The Discarded Image* (Cambridge University Press,
1964).

This book translates many background texts:
R. P. Miller (ed.), *Chaucer: Sources and Backgrounds* (Oxford
University Press, 1977).

This article discusses the astrological dating of *The Nun's
Priest's Tale*:
J. D. North, 'Kalenderes Enlumyned ben they', *Review of
English Studies* 20 (1969), pp. 418–44.

These articles analyse the sources of the tale:
R. A. Pratt, 'Three Old French Sources of the *Nonnes Preestes
Tale*', *Speculum* 47 (1972), pp. 422–44, 646–68.
R. A. Pratt, 'Some Latin Sources of the Nonnes Preest on
Dreams', *Speculum* 52 (1977), pp. 538–70.

This book reprints contemporary documents relating to four-teenth-century life:
E. Rickert (ed.), *Chaucer's World* (Columbia University Press, 1948).

This page of the Luminarium website gives access to essays on *The Canterbury Tales*, including *The Nun's Priest's Tale*. This sector of the luminarium website offers useful materials on medieval literature:
www.luminarium.org/medlit/chaucessays.htm

This page gives access to a range of excellent teaching and scholarly materials on Chaucer:
www.courses.fas.harvard.edu/~chaucer/index.ht

Language

D. Burnley, *A Guide to Chaucer's Language* (Methuen, 1983).

A Note on Chaucer's English

Chaucer's English has so many similarities with Modern English that it is unnecessary to learn extensive tables of grammar. With a little practice, and using the glosses provided, it should not be too difficult to read the text. Nevertheless, it would be foolish to pretend that there are no differences. The remarks which follow offer some information, hints and principles to assist students who are reading Chaucer's writings for the first time, and to illustrate some of the differences (and some of the similarities) between Middle and Modern English. More comprehensive and systematic treatments of this topic are available in *The Riverside Chaucer* and in D. Burnley, *A Guide to Chaucer's Language*.

1 Inflections

These are changes or additions to words, usually endings, which provide information about number (whether a verb or a noun is singular or plural), tense or gender.

a) Verbs

In the **present** tense most verbs add –e in the first person singular (e.g. *I rede*), –est in the second person singular (*thou biwreyest*), –eth in the third person singular (*he clymbeth*) and –en in the plural. This can be summarized as follows:

	Middle English	Modern English
Singular	1 I telle 2 Thou tellest 3 He/She/It telleth	I tell You tell He/She/It tells
Plural	1 We tellen 2 Ye tellen 3 They tellen	We tell You tell They tell

As you can see, Middle English retains more inflections than Modern English, but the system is simple enough. Old English, the phase of the language between around 449 AD, when the Angles first came to Britain, and about 1100, had many more inflections.

In describing the **past** tense it is necessary to begin by making a distinction, which still applies in Modern English, between strong and weak verbs. **Strong verbs** form their past tense by changing their stem (e.g. I sing, I sang; you drink, you drank; he fights, he fought; we throw, we threw), while **weak verbs** add to the stem (I want, I wanted; you laugh, you laughed; he dives, he dived).

Strong verbs		
	Middle English Present stem: 'sing'	**Modern English**
Singular	1 I sange (or soonge) 2 Thou songe 3 He/She/It sange	I sang (or sung) You sang He/She/It sang
Plural	1 We songen 2 Ye songen 3 They songen	We sang You sang They sang
Weak verbs		
	Middle English Present stem: 'here'	**Modern English**
Singular	1 I herde 2 Thou herdest 3 He/She/It herde	I heard You heard He/She/It heard
Plural	1 We herden 2 Ye herden 3 They herden	We heard You heard They heard

In the past tense in Middle English, strong verbs change their stems (e.g. *sing* becomes *sang* or *song*) and add −e in the second person singular (e.g. *thou songe*) and −en in the plural (e.g. *they songen*). Weak verbs add −de or −te (e.g. *fele* becomes *felte*, *here* becomes *herde*) with −st in the second person singular (e.g. *thou herdest*) and −n in the plural (e.g. *they felten*). The table on page 000 compares the past tense in Middle and Modern English for strong and weak verbs.

The past tense can also be formed using the auxiliary verb *gan* plus the past participle (e.g. *gan gronen*: groaned [120], *gan... calle*: called [237]). In a few cases *gan* means 'began', particularly in phrases involving the preposition 'to' (e.g. *gan to rynge*: began to ring [*The Miller's Tale*, 547]) but the past is preferable in every instance in *The Nun Priest's Tale*. Some verbs add initial y to make their past participle (e.g. *yronne*: run [428], *ywarned*: warned [466]).

b) Nouns and adjectives

Nouns mostly add −s or −es in the plural (e.g. *belles* [28], but notice *clerkis* [469]) and possessive (e.g. *Poules* [14]). There are no apostrophes in Middle English! (But modern editors sometimes add one to indicate that a letter has been elided, e.g. *N'apoplexie* [75].) Some nouns add −en in the plural (e.g. *doghtren*: daughters [63]). Although (unlike modern French or German) nouns do not take grammatical gender in Middle English, some nouns do add −e in the feminine. Some adjectives add −e in the plural. Some adjectives are converted to adverbs by the addition of −e (e.g. *faire*: elegantly [441]).

c) Personal pronouns

The forms of the personal pronouns are somewhat different from those used in Modern English and are worth recording in full:

		Subject	**Object**	**Possessive**
Singular	1	I, ich	me	myn, my
	2	Thou, thow	thee	Thyn, thy
	3 masculine	He	hym, him	his
	3 feminine	She	her	hir, hire
	3 neuter	It, hit	it, hit	his
Plural	1	We	us	owre, our, owres
	2	Ye	you, yow	your, youres
	3	They	hem	hire, here

Remember that the distinction between *thou* and *you* in Middle English often involves politeness and social relationship as well as number. This is similar to modern French or German. Thus *thou* forms are used with friends, family and social inferiors, *you* forms with strangers or superiors. In *The Nun's Priest's Tale Prologue*, The Host uses *you* to The Monk and *thou* to The Nun's Priest.

2 Relative pronouns

The main **relative pronouns** found are *that* and *which*. In translating *that* it is often wise to try out a range of Modern English equivalents, such as *who*, *whom*, *which*. The prefix *ther–* in such words as *therto* and *therwith* often refers back to the subject matter of the previous phrase. *Therto* may be translated as 'in addition to all that' or 'in order to achieve that'.

3 Impersonal construction

With certain verbs the **impersonal construction** is quite common (e.g. *bifel*: it happened [116], *Hym thoughte*: it seemed to him [245], *Hym mette*: he dreamed [312], *it reweth me*: it saddens me [331]).

4 Reflexive pronouns

Many verbs can be used with a **reflexive pronoun**, a pronoun which refers back to the subject (as in modern French or German) and which may, depending on the verb employed, be translated or understood as part of the verb (e.g. *Ye purge yow*: you purge yourself [181], *peyne hym*: take pains [539]).

5 Extra negatives

In Middle English extra **negatives** often make the negative stronger, whereas in Modern English double negatives cancel each other out. *I noot nevere what* (17) would now be 'I have no idea at all what', *Nothyng ne liste hym* (510) 'He had no wish at all', *ne was ther no* (571) 'there was no'.

6 Contraction

Sometimes negatives and pronouns merge with their associated verbs (e.g. *noot* [= *ne woot*]: do not know [17], *maistow*: you may [340], *woldestow*: would you [580]).

7 Word order

Middle English **word order** is often freer than Modern English, and in particular there is more inversion of subject and verb (e.g. *Ran Colle oure dogge* [617]) or subject and complement (e.g. *Ful is myn herte* [437]). In analysing difficult sentences you should first locate the verb, then its subject, then the object or complement. (Roughly, a verb which involves activity takes an object – she hit the ball, he gave her the book – while a verb which describes a state of affairs takes a complement – it was yellow, you look better.) Then you should put these elements together. It should then be easier to see how the various qualifiers fit in.

In line 537 the main verb is 'was'. When we put this with its subject and complement we reach: 'it came from the heart'. The second phrase (*al that he song*) can then be used as a subject for the main verb, and a position can be found for the qualifier: 'certainly everything that he sung **came from the heart**'.

Sometimes problems are caused by the way in which several phrases are joined into a single complex sentence. In the sentence beginning at line 538 the main clause links two verbal phrases *wolde... peyne him* (539) and *moste wynke* (540): 'he would make such an effort that he had to close both his eyes'. Two of the remaining clauses elaborate his intentions: *And for to make his voys the moore strong* and *so loude he wolde cryen*. The rest of the sentence describes his other physical contortions (541–2). The sentence which results turns back on itself more than a modern teacher would really like, but it makes perfect sense: 'And in order to make his voice stronger, **he would make such an effort that he had to close both his eyes**, because he wanted to sing so loud, and in addition he would stand on his tiptoes and stretch out his long thin neck'. Perhaps the contortion suits the fox's devious attempts to trick Chauntecleer. Similar problems can arise from phrases being added on to sentences without sufficient explanation. In the sentence beginning at line 533, the main idea is expressed in the final clause: 'I never heard anyone sing as well as your father did in the morning'. The awkwardness comes from the addition of two phrases of preparation and an inserted oath (534), but the meaning remains reasonably clear: 'But if we are on the subject of singing I will say (as I may continue to enjoy the use of both my eyes) that, apart from you, **I never heard anyone sing as well as your father did in the morning.**'

8 Connection of clauses

Middle English often does not indicate **connection of clauses** as clearly as Modern English. In seeking to understand or in translating you may need to provide connecting words (as I did in the discussion of the sentences in the previous section). On occasion you may have to provide verbs which have been omitted, particularly the verb 'to be' – e.g. *this my conclusioun*: this is my conclusion (291) – or verbs of motion. You may also need to regularize number or tense (in some Middle English sentences a subject can shift from singular to plural or a verb from present to past).

Chaucer can mix the past tense with the historic present (sometimes in telling a story we use the present tense, even though we and our audience know that the events occurred in the past) but a Modern English writer would have to maintain consistency at least within the sentence and usually within the paragraph as well. Chaucer's usage here (and with the implied words and the lack of connectives) may well be closer to spoken English than modern formal writing could be.

9 Change of meaning

Although most of the words which Chaucer uses are still current (often with different spellings) in Modern English, some of them have changed their meaning. So it is a good idea to check the Notes or the Glossary even for the words which look familiar. If you are interested in investigating the ways in which words change their meanings over time you can look at the quotations provided in large historical dictionaries, such as the *Oxford English Dictionary* or the *Shorter Oxford Dictionary* or in R. W. Burchfield, *The English Language* (Oxford, 1985), pp. 113–23, or G. Hughes, *Words in Time: A Social History of English Vocabulary* (Oxford, Blackwell). Some examples from *The Nun's Priest's Tale* are shown in the table on p. 146.

Middle English	(line number)	Meaning	Equivalent modern word
actes	(370)	histories	acts
bord	(77)	table	board
buxom	(n. 148)	obedient	buxom
cas	(438)	chance, fortune	case
casuelly	(335)	by chance	casually
clerk	(470)	student, learned man	clerk
clos	(594)	yard, enclosure	close
compleccioun	(158)	temperament	complexion
congregacioun	(222)	gathering, crowd	congregation
conseil	(487, 522)	secret, advice	counsel
corage	(686)	heart, sexual desire	courage
countrefete	(555)	imitate	counterfeit
debonaire	(105)	gracious, modest	debonair
deel	(349)	part	deal
estaat	(9)	position in society, status	estate, state
gentil	(99)	noble, highborn, virtuous	gentle

n. = cited in note to this line

A Note on Pronunciation

The Nun's Priest's Tale, like other poems, benefits from being read aloud. Even if you read it aloud in a Modern English pronunciation you will get more from it, but Middle English was pronounced differently (the sounds of a language change at least as much as the vocabulary or the constructions) and it helps to make some attempt at a Middle English accent. The best way to learn this is to imitate one of the recordings (those issued by Pavilion and Argo are especially recommended for this purpose). A few principles are given below; more can be found in *The Riverside Chaucer*.

1   In most cases you should pronounce all consonants (e.g. you should sound the 'k' in knight and the 'l' in half). But in words of French origin initial 'h' (e.g. as in *herbes* [183]) should not be sounded, nor should 'g' in the combination 'gn'. The combination 'gh' (as in *right* [2]) is best sounded 'ch' as Scottish 'loch'.

2   In most cases all vowels are sounded, though a final 'e' may be silent because of elision with a vowel following (e.g. do not sound the 'e' in *namoore of* [1]) or because of the stress pattern of the line (e.g. I would sound the final 'e' in *muche* [4], but leave it silent in *moore* [3]).

3   Two points of spelling affect pronunciation. When 'y' appears as a vowel you should sound it as 'i' (see table on p. 148). Sometimes a 'u' sound before 'n' or 'm' was written 'o' (because 'u' and 'n' look very similar in the handwriting of the time). This means that *song* and *yong* should be pronounced 'sung' and 'yung'. This also applies in *comen* and *sone* (as in their Modern English equivalents 'come' and 'son').

4 You will not go too far wrong with combinations of vowels, such as *ai*, *eu* and *oy* if you sound them as in Modern English. There are significant exceptions (e.g. *hous* [531], and many words with a similar ending should be pronounced with an *oo* sound) but it is not possible to establish reliable rules purely on the basis of the spelling.

5 The principal vowel sounds differ somewhat from Modern English. They are set out in the table below (adapted from Norman Davis's table in *The Riverside Chaucer*). The table distinguishes long and short versions of each vowel. This distinction still applies in Modern English (consider the 'a' sounds in *hat* and *father*) but unfortunately it is often only possible to decide whether a particular vowel is long or short by knowing about the derivation of the word. Do not despair. Even a rough approximation will help you. Only experts in medieval languages have reliable Middle English accents, and even they cannot be sure that Chaucer would have approved them.

Vowel	Middle English example	Modern equivalent sound
Long 'a'	name (26), cas (438)	'a' in father
Short 'a'	nat (48), sat (118)	'a' in hat
Long 'e'	she (107), been (125)	'a' in fate
Open 'e'	deeth (583), breche (682)	'e' in there
Short 'e'	gentil (99), wende (315)	'e' in set
Unstressed 'e'	nones (567), sonne (112)	'a' in about, 'e' in forgotten
Long 'i'	I (114), tyme (114)	'i' in machine
Short 'i'	hym (102), aright (130)	'i' in sit
Long 'o'	no (149), moot (50)	'o' in note
Open 'o'	hooly (353)	'oa' in broad
Short 'o'	som (177), solas (404)	'o' in hot
Long 'u'	hous (531)	'oo' in boot
Short 'u'	but (156), ful (168)	'u' in put

Glossary

This glossary is not absolutely comprehensive. It does not record all inflected forms (see A Note on Chaucer's English, p. 139) nor all variant spellings. If you do not find a word here, try sounding it out, or try minor modifications of spelling (such as 'i' for 'y', 'a' for 'o', 'ea' for 'ee', and vice versa). Generally the main meaning in this text comes first while more specialized meanings are given line references. Proper names which are explained in the Notes do not appear in the glossary. In compiling this glossary I have used the editions mentioned under Further Reading, especially Sisam's, and L. D. Benson (ed.), *The Riverside Chaucer* and N. Davis (ed.), *A Chaucer Glossary*, which offer fuller explanations than I can here. I have also consulted the *Oxford English Dictionary* and *The Middle English Dictionary*.

abhomynable unnatural, hateful
abideth remains
abrayde started, woke suddenly
abyde remain, wait
accord harmony
accordant to in keeping with
actes histories
adversitee trouble
aferd afraid
affermeth upholds the truth of
affrayed afraid
afright frightened
after after, afterwards, for (262), according to (469)
agast afraid
agaste frighten
agayn towards, facing
ago gone
agon gone

agrief amiss, unkindly
agu ague, acute fever
alday continually
als also
also as (445)
altercacioun disagreement
amended bettered
anhanged hung
anon at once, immediately
anoyeth wearies, displeases
apothecarie pharmacist, seller of herbal cures
areest arrest, seizure
aright correctly, favourably, truly
arrayed arranged, disposed
arresten seize
arwes arrows
ascencioun ascension (see Note, p. 00, lines 89–92)

assaille assail, attack
asure lapis lazuli (a blue stone)
attamed begun
atte at
attempree moderate
auctorite authority
auctour author
availle profit, be of use
avaunter boaster
aventure chance, lot, events that happen
avisioun prophetic dream, a vision

bad advised
bane death
bar hyrself conducted herself
bataille battle
batailled crenellated, in the shape of battlements
bathe hire immerse herself, rub herself
beer carried
bemes beams
bemes trumpets (632)
bene bean
benefice church job
berd beard
beres bears
be stille leave alone
bifel it happened
biforn before
bigyle deceive, beguile
biknewe acknowledged, confessed
bisyde alongside
bitwixe between
biwaille bewail, cry
biwreyest reveal
blak, blake black

blis happiness
blisful blessed, holy, happy, joyful
blithe happy
boles bulls
boon bone
bord table
boterflye butterfly
botme bottom
bour bower, bedroom
box boxwood
bras brass
brasile brazil wood (bright-red dye)
brast broke
braunes muscles
breche buttocks
breeke would burst
bren bran
brend burned
brouke use
bulte boult, sift
burned burnished
but but, unless, except, only
butiller butler, steward
buxom obedient
byde wait
byle bill
bynethe beneath

carter cart-driver, carrier
cas chance, fortune
casten hem planned
casuelly by chance
catel property
cause reason, purpose (302)
centaure lesser centaury (herb)
certes certainly
chaf husk

cherl churl, peasant, rogue
chide reproach
chirche church
chuk cluck
clappeth chatters, babbles
clepe call
clerk educated man, scholar
clokke clock
cloos closed
clos yard, enclosure
clynkyng tinkling
colde disastrous, fatal
colera choler (see Note, p. 49, line 162)
coleryk choleric
col-fox fox with black markings
commune common
compaignable companionable, friendly
compaignye company
complecciouns temperaments
compleyne lament
compleynedest lamented
condicioneel conditional
congregacioun gathering, crowd
conseil advice (487), secrets (522)
conseille advise
contek strife
contrarie opposite, enemy, against (303)
contree country
coomb comb
corage heart, sexual desire
corn grain
cote shelter, cottage
countrefete imitate
cours voyage, journey

crew crowed
cronycle chronicle, history
crye out on appeal to

dale valley
damoysele damsel, lady
daun master, sir
dawenynge dawn
debonaire gracious, modest
deed dead
deel part
delit delight, enjoyment
delyverly quickly, nimbly
departen part
desport entertainment, pleasure
devyse describe
deye die
deye dairywoman (80)
deyntee choice, delicious
diffye reject, scorn, repudiate
discrecioun understanding, sound judgement
discreet wise, kind
disese sorrow, pain
disputisoun debate
dissymulour deceiver
divyne guess, suppose
doctrine instruction, teaching
doghtren daughters
dokes ducks
dong dung
dorste dare
doutelees undoubtedly
drecched troubled
drede fear
dreynt drowned
dwelle remain, delay
dyde died
dyen die

dystaf distaff, spinning stick
(see Note, p. 78, line 618)

eek also
eeris ears
effect consequence
ellebor black hellebore (herb)
elles else
endite write
engendren are caused
engyned racked, tormented
ensamples examples
entente intention, purpose
equinoxial equinoctial (see
Note, p. 42, lines 89–92)
er before
erly early
erst before
eschewed escaped, avoided
ese ease, prosperity
espye see, spy out
estaat state, social position
even-tyde evening
everichon every one
evermo always
expowned explained,
interpreted
ey egg
eyen eyes
eyled afflicted
eyleth troubles, afflicts

fader father
faire beautiful, gracious,
beautifully, well
falle fall, happen, occur, befall,
pounce
faren gone
fayn gladly
feend devil

feere fear
felawe friend, companion
felonye felony, serious crime
fer far
fered frightened
fethered clasped with his wings
fil befell
flatour flatterer
flee fly
fleigh flew
fley flew
floures flowers
flowen flew
folye foolish thing, trifle
foond found, provided
forncast planned beforehand
fors force, importance
forslewthen waste through
idleness
fortunat prosperous, favoured
by the goddess Fortune
forwityng foreknowledge
forwoot foreknows, foreknew
(482)
fre generous, noble
fresshe new, young, blooming
fro from
ful very, much
fume exhalations, vapours
fumetere fumitory (herb)
fy fie (exclamation of dismay:
'how could you')
fyn fine

gabbe lie
gaitrys (?) buckthorn (herb)
game sport, enjoyment, joke
gan did (indicates past tense:
see A Note on Chaucer's
English, p. 139)

gapyng with mouth open wide
gargat throat
gentil noble
gentillesse nobility, kindness
gesse guess, suppose
gilt guilt
glade gladden
gladly usually, willingly
gladsom pleasing
governaunce control, self-control
graunt mercy many thanks
greet great
gret large
gronen groan
grote groat (obsolete coin; see Note, p. 51, line 192)
grove copse, small wood
grym fierce

habundant abundant
han have
happed it happened
hardy bold
harrow cry of distress
haven harbour
heed head
heeld held, considered
heeris hairs
hegges hedges
heigh high, noble
hele good health
heled concealed
hem them
hent seized
herbergage accommodation
herbe yve (?)buckthorn
herde heard
herkne listen
herte heart

hertelees heartless, coward
hertely heartily
hevene heaven, the sky (432)
hevynesse sadness, sorrow
hewe colour
hewed coloured
hight(e) named, was called
hir, hire her
hir, hire their
holde in treat with
holden consider
hoo stop
hoold keeping, possession
hooly holy, pure, innocent
hoote hot
hostelrye lodging
hostiler innkeeper
hound dog
housbondrye husbandry, household management
howped whooped
hydous frightful, hideous

in inn, lodging
iniquitee deceitful wickedness

jangleth talks, chatters
japes deceptions, tricks
jeet jet
jolif cheerful

kan can, know how to
katapuce caper spurge (herb)
keen cows
keep notice
kepe protect, preserve
konne can
koude knew how to
kyn kin, family
kynde nature

lat let
lawriol spurge laurel (herb)
laxatyf laxative
leere learn
legende biography of a saint
lemes flames
leoun lion
lese lose
leste it pleased
lette hinder, prevent, delay (268, 318)
leve leave
levere rather
leye lay, bet
lief love, dear
liggen lie
lightly quickly
liste pleased
lite, litel little
lith lies
lith limb (109)
lo look, consider, see
logge lodging
loken locked
lond land, country
loore learning
lorn lost
losengeour flatterer, deceiver
lust desire
lye lie
lyf life, biography
lyte small, little

maad made
maistow may you
malencolie melancholy
man one, anyone (121, 512, 535)
maner kind of
mateere matter, subject

maugree in spite of
maze delusion, source of bewilderment
mente meant
mervaille marvel, wonder
mery pleasant
meschaunce mischance
meschief trouble, misfortune
messe-dayes days when mass is given, feast days
met, mette dreamed
meynee crowd, rabble
ministres magistrates
moo more
moot might, must (468)
moralite moral lesson
mordre murder
mordrour murderer
morwe morning
mosten must
muche much, many (4)
muchel much
multiplye increase the population
murie joyful, musical, tuneful
myght strength
myn my, mine
myrie merry, happy, pleasantly situated (305)
myschaunce misfortune

namo no more
namoore no more
narwe narrow, small
nas was not
nat not
natheless nonetheless
ne not, nor, neither
nedely necessarily
nedes necessarily

neer nearer
nekke neck
nekke-bon neck
nere were it not for
newe recently
nones purpose, occasion
noon none, no
noot do not know
norice nurse
notabilitee point to note
ny nigh, near
nyce foolish
nygard miser

o one, same (310)
of by (382, 590), about (563)
ofter more often
ones once
orgon organs
orlogge clock
out help (exclamation of distress, 614)
outrely utterly, completely

paramour mistress, lover
pardee by God
parfit perfect, educated
passe pass, go, surpass (545)
passe over leave aside, move on
pasture the act of feeding
peer equal
pees peace, silence
perche perch
pestilence plague
peyne pain, suffering
peyne hym take pains, make an effort
phisik medicine
pitous piteous, sad

pleasance pleasure
pleye play, sexual activity
pleyne lament
point detail
povre poor
powped puffed
poynaunt sharp, spicy
preeve proof
preye beg, ask
prisoun prison, captivity
prively secretly
prow profit, benefit
pryme prime (9 a.m.)
pyned tortured

quelle kill
quod said

rad read
rage frenzy, violent grief
ravysshed overcome, seduced
real royal, regal
recche interpret
reccheless heedless, careless
rede, reed read
reed red (76, 136, 395)
regnes kingdoms
rekke care
remedie help, consolation
remes countries
rennen run
renoun renown, fame
rente tore (335)
rente income
repaire go
repleccioun excess, over-eating (71)
repleet full
reported told
rethor expert in rhetoric

Glossary

revel pleasure
reweth saddens
right quite, very much, just, exactly
roghte care about, pay attention to
rometh roams, walks
ronne ran
roore roar

saufly safely
saugh saw
save apart from
say saw
sayn say
scole university
secree discreet
seculer secular (see Note, p. 84, line 684)
see sea (301, 504)
seinte holy
seith says, tells (593)
seken seek, search
sely poor, simple
sentence meaning, opinion, subject-matter (448), intelligence (584)
sette value, place
sewed followed, pursued
seyd said
seye say
seyled sailed
seyn say
seyn seen (595)
seynd singed, grilled
shaltow you shall
shente injured, ruined
sherte shirt
shoon shone
shrewe beshrew, curse

shrighte shrieked
significaciouns indications, signs
siker sure, certain, reliable
sikerer more certain, more reliable
sikerly certainly
sith since
sklendre thin, meagre
skriked shrieked
slawe slain
slough mud
sly deceitful
smal small, slim (139)
so so, so much, as
sodeyn sudden
solas comfort, pleasure
somdeel somewhat
sondry different
sone son
sonne sun
soond sand
soore sorely, severely
sooth truth, truly
soothfastnesse truth
sore severely
sorwe sorrow
sorweful lamentable
soverayn, sovereyn chief, supreme
spak spoke
sperhauk sparrowhawk
sprynge rise, blossom, sprout
stape advanced
staves sticks
stedefast resolute
sterte leaped, rushed
stevene voice
stikkes stakes
stirte leap, rush

stoon testicle (682)
stoor stock, value, trust
streit narrow, shortage (223)
streite drawn (591)
streyneth constrains
strook stroke
stynte stop
substance essence, heart of the matter
subtiltee ingenuity
suffisaunce contentment
suffre allow
superfluytee superfluity, excess
sustre sister
swevene dream
swich such
syde side, edge (645)
syen see
syn since

taak take
tale tale, speech (316), significance (352)
tarie delay, wait
techen show, teach
terciane tertian (a fever which becomes stronger every other day)
thane then
thee you, prosper (210, 666)
ther there, where
therwith at that, with that, in addition (527)
therwithal at that, in addition
thilke the same, that
tho those
thridde third
thritty thirty
thurghout through
thynketh thinks, seems

tiptoon tiptoes
to to, too
tomorwe tomorrow
tool weapon
toon toes
torment anguish (600)
touchyng concerning
toun town
trad trod, copulated with
traisoun treason
trede-foul lover of hens, lecher
trespas injury, wrong
trete of deal with, treat
tribulaciouns troubles
turned hym turned over
tweye two
twies twice
tyde time

undiscreet careless, foolish
undren undern (mid-morning)
unwar unexpected
up upon (178)
upright upwards (276)

vanitee emptiness, foolishness
venymes poisons
verray true, fine
veyn vain
viage journey, voyage
vileynye discourtesy

war aware
ware beware
wel well, very, much, happy (110)
wende go
werken work, cause (172)
wexeth becomes
weylaway woe, alas

whelpes dogs
wher whether
whilom once
whit white
wight person, creature
wikke evil, wicked
wilfully deliberately, perversely
wise manner, way
withoute outside
witnesse take evidence from
wityng knowledge
wlatsom revolting
wo sorrow
wode wood
woful sorrowful
wolde would, wanted,
    intended (521)
woldestow would you
wole will
wolt will
wonder strange (312)
woned lived, remained
wonne won, captured
wont accustomed
wook woke
woot knows

wortes vegetables, cabbages
wroght created
wydwe widow
wyf wife
wynke close the eyes
wys wise
wys certainly, surely (642)

yaf gave
ydoon done
ye you
ye yes
yeerd yard, enclosed garden
yet still
yis yes
ylogged lodged
ymaginacioun imagination (see
    Note, p. 66, line 451)
ynough enough
yolleden screeched
yow you
yronne run
yseyled sailed
ywarned warned
ywis indeed
ywrite written

Appendix

The description of The Prioress

(See p. 6 for an illustration of The Prioress.) In the *General Prologue*, The Nun's Priest is merely named as one among three priests accompanying The Prioress, so there can be no question of comparing his tale with his description. But his tale does deal with topics raised in her description from the *General Prologue* (diet, the appropriateness of noble behaviour, the love of animals) and it expresses opinions about the relations between the sexes, so it may be interesting to make comparisons between *The Nun's Priest's Tale* and this famous description of The Prioress. The Prioress appears to be of noble birth. Her name, her table-manners, her behaviour, and her appearance imitate the descriptions of heroines in romances. Many of her actions (such as going on pilgrimages, wearing fashionable clothes, and keeping dogs) are, by medieval standards, unsuited to a nun. Nonetheless, Chaucer's narrator appears to be overwhelmed by admiration for her. There is a full discussion of this description in the Oxford Student Texts edition of the *General Prologue to the Canterbury Tales*.

> Ther was also a Nonne, a PRIORESSE,
> That of hir smylyng was ful symple and coy;
> 120   Hire gretteste ooth was but by Seinte Loy;
> And she was cleped madame Eglentyne.
> Ful weel she soong the service dyvyne,
> Entuned in hir nose ful semely;
> And Frenssh she spak ful faire and fetisly,
> 125   After the scole of Stratford atte Bowe,
> For Frenssh of Parys was to hire unknowe.
> At mete wel ytaught was she with alle;
> She leet no morsel from hir lippes falle,
> Ne wette hir fyngres in hir sauce depe;
> 130   Wel koude she carie a morsel and wel kepe

That no drope ne fille upon hire brest.
In curteisie was set ful muchel hir lest.
Hir over-lippe wyped she so clene
That in hir coppe ther was no ferthyng sene
135   Of grece, whan she dronken hadde hir draughte.
Ful semely after hir mete she raughte.
And sikerly she was of greet desport,
And ful plesaunt, and amyable of port,
And peyned hire to countrefete cheere
140   Of court, and to been estatlich of manere,
And to ben holden digne of reverence.
But for to speken of hire conscience,
She was so charitable and so pitous
She wolde wepe, if that she saugh a mous
145   Kaught in a trappe, if it were deed or bledde.
Of smale houndes hadde she that she fedde
With rosted flessh, or milk and wastel-breed.
But soore wepte she if oon of hem were deed,
Or if men smoot it with a yerde smerte;
150   And al was conscience and tendre herte.
Ful semyly hir wympul pynched was,
Hir nose tretys, hir eyen greye as glas,
Hir mouth ful smal, and therto softe and reed.
But sikerly she hadde a fair forheed;
155   It was almost a spanne brood, I trowe;
For, hardily, she was nat undergrowe.
Ful fetys was hir cloke, as I was war.
Of smal coral aboute hire arm she bar
A peire of bedes, gauded al with grene,
160   And theron heng a brooch of gold ful sheene,
On which ther was first write a crowned A,
And after *Amor vincit omnia.*
      Another NONNE with hire hadde she,
That was hir chapeleyne, and preestes thre.

(*General Prologue*, 118–64)

119 **symple and coy** innocent and quiet   120 **gretteste ooth**
strongest oath   **Seinte Loy** St Eligius   121 **cleped** called
123 **Entuned** intoned   124 **fetisly** elegantly   130 **kepe** ensure
132 **lest** pleasure   133 **over-lippe** upper lip   134 **ferthyng** speck
136 **semely**   graciously **raughte** reached   137 **of greet desport**
very merry   138 **port** manner   139 **countrefete cheere** imitate
the behaviour   141 **digne** worthy   143 **pitous** compassionate
147 **flessh** meat **wastel-breed** high-quality bread   149 **smoot**
struck **yerde** stick **smerte** painfully   151 **wympul** head-dress
pynched pleated   152 **tretys** well-formed   155 **spanne brood**
18–23 cm wide   159 **gauded** divided   160 **sheene** bright
161 **write** written   162 *Amor vincit omnia* (Latin) Love conquers
all.

Chauntecleer's first story

According to R. A. Pratt (see Notes, p. 54) Chaucer drew on three different versions of this story. This version from Cicero's Latin prose treatise *De divinatione* (written about 44 BC) was the earliest of the ones Chaucer used. You may want to compare this version of the story with the way Chauntecleer tells it (see lines 218–96).

> Two friends from Arcadia were travelling together and had come to Megara. One went to stay with an innkeeper, the other with a friend. After eating they went to sleep. The one who was staying with a friend dreamt that he saw his fellow traveller begging him to come and help because he was about to be killed by the innkeeper. Terrified the dreamer rose from his first sleep. Then when he had collected himself and concluded that his dream had no value he went back to sleep. Then his friend appeared again to the dreamer to ask him that, even if he would not help him while he was still alive, at least he would not allow his death to remain unavenged. He said that once he had been killed he had been placed in a cart by the innkeeper and covered over with dung. He asked his friend to go to the city gate early in the morning before the cart could leave the city. His friend was troubled by this dream and in the morning went to the gate, where there was a ploughman waiting to go out. The friend asked him what was in the cart. Terrified, the ploughman ran away. The dead man was discovered and the innkeeper paid the penalty for the crime he had committed.
>
> (translated from Cicero, *De divinatione*, 1. 57.)

A beast-fable from Aesop

This is one of the best known of all beast-fables. It is referred to by the Roman poet Horace in *Satires*, II, 5 (about 30 BC) and is the second fable of the seventeenth-century French poet La Fontaine. You might like to consider how this typical beast-fable works and how Chaucer draws on this form but also develops its possibilities.

> A Crow sits in a tree eating some meat. A hungry Fox approaches. He praises the Crow's beautiful feathers and says that the Crow would be the best of birds if only it could sing. The Crow opens his mouth to sing, letting fall the meat, which the crafty Fox eats up.

A summary of the story of Reynard and Chantecler

The story of Chantecler is only one episode in the Old French Beast Epic the *Roman de Renart*, a cycle of stories which began to circulate in the late twelfth century and which reached its present form around 1250. The main parts (or branches) of the *Roman de Renart* have been translated by D. D. R. Owen as *The Romance of Reynard the Fox* (World's Classics, 1994). Chaucer certainly used this version of the story. You might like to think about how Chaucer has adapted his source.

> Reynard, the rascally fox who is always full of tricks, wants to enter the farm of Constant des Noues, a wealthy peasant who owns many hens, cocks, ducks and geese, but Constant has protected his farmyard with a fence. Eventually Reynard manages to enter because one of the stakes is broken, and hides in the cabbage patch. The hens notice him and are afraid.
>
> The cockerel Chantecler asks his hens why they are running away. Pinte, the wisest of the hens, explains that they have seen a wild beast. Chantecler laughs at their fear and returns to his perch on a dunghill where he falls asleep. He dreams that a creature wearing a red cloak with a collar of bones rushes at him. The creature forces him to put on the cloak which is tight around his neck and hurts him. Chantecler is so frightened that he wakes up and goes to tell Pinte about his dream.
>
> She explains that the animal in the dream must be the fox. The tight collar of bone must be his mouth with its teeth. She interprets the dream to mean that the fox will catch Chantecler before noon, but he laughs at her because he is confident that no fox can get through the fence around the farmyard. He returns to his dunghill and goes back to sleep.
>
> The fox approaches and pounces at Chantecler but misses him. Then Reynard decides to trick him instead. 'Don't run

away', he says, 'we are cousins. Do you remember how beautifully your father used to sing. He could hold a high note for a long time when he sang with both his eyes closed.' At first Chantecler suspects the fox's intentions, but eventually he is flattered into singing. As soon as he shuts his eyes Reynard seizes him and carries him off.

Pinte is grief-stricken. The farmer's wife raises the alarm and the farm servants and the dogs join in the pursuit. Chantecler is done for unless he can think of a trick. He urges Reynard to defy the rabble chasing them.

No one is so wise that they never make a mistake and Reynard the trickster was tricked this time. He shouted, 'I'm taking this one off and there is nothing you can do about it.' As soon as Reynard opened his mouth, Chantecler escaped. Reynard was furious and cursed his talkativeness. Chantecler blamed himself for shutting his eyes when he should have remained vigilant. Reynard rushed off into the woods, sad and angry at missing a meal.

(summarized from the *Roman de Renart*, Branch II, Lines 1–468, printed in W. F. Bryan and G. Dempster (eds), *Sources and Analogues of Chaucer's Canterbury Tales* [Humanities Press, 1958], pp. 646–58.)